"I'm looking forward to working with you."

His voice was seductive. "I think you'll be terrific."

Bella was mesmerized by him. "I hope so." She tossed her hair gently. "Mauritius sounds wonderful."

"I'm sure it will be wonderful." His voice was a low deep rasp. "There's just one tiny little thing...."

A cold ripple of apprehension went through Bella as she saw his gaze grow black. Too late, she realized she'd been led into a trap.

"It's this." His voice was harsh. "You might be a terrific little seductress. You certainly like using your eyes and mouth and all those other bits God gave you, but just remember, it's your acting skills I'm hiring, not your flirting ones. And I expect you to remember that every single day you work for me."

Carol Gregor is married with two children and works as a journalist. She lists her hobbies as "reading, first and foremost, followed by eating and drinking with friends, gardening and films. I am also a private pilot, but a lapsed one since becoming a mother!"

Books by Carol Gregor

HARLEQUIN ROMANCE
2732—LORD OF THE AIR

HARLEQUIN PRESENTS
1074—MARRY IN HASTE
1129—THE TRUSTING HEART
1338—BITTER SECRET

PRETENCE OF LOVE
Carol Gregor

Harlequin Books

TORONTO • NEW YORK • LONDON
AMSTERDAM • PARIS • SYDNEY • HAMBURG
STOCKHOLM • ATHENS • TOKYO • MILAN

Original hardcover edition published in 1990
by Mills & Boon Limited

ISBN 0-373-03124-6

Harlequin Romance first edition May 1991

PRETENCE OF LOVE

CHAPTER ONE

BELLA swallowed hard and knocked on the door marked 'Picture Promotions.'

'Come.'

The voice sounded so curt that her courage nearly deserted her. She licked her lips and felt her tongue slide silkily over the unaccustomed lip gloss that covered them.

'Yep?'

The man had his back to her and stared down into the busy West End street below as he listened intently to the phone held to his ear. He half turned to nod at a chair before continuing his conversation. Then the call was finished, and he swung round to her, slapping the cordless receiver down into his other palm with aggressive, restless energy.

She took one look at him and her mouth went dry and her mind cried 'Help!' in a silent plea of desperation. He was tall, lithe and so powerfully handsome that she felt her legs start to shake as his eyes scoured over her.

She had heard of people being bowled over, but she had never believed it. Until now, that was, when the simple force of his presence seemed almost enough to knock her off her feet. Certainly it was enough to blow to the four winds the fragile shreds of self-confidence that she had managed to gather around her as she had walked slowly up the stairs to his office.

She would never carry it off, she thought despairingly. He was quite clearly nobody's fool. But she had to, she just had to! So she stood firm, and dragged her eyes from his so she could look around the room while she struggled to regain composure.

The office was a chaos of paper and jangling phones, which he ignored.

'Hell's teeth, what a day!'

Bella's eyes were drawn back to his by the deep vibrancy of his voice. He put a foot up on a chair and ran a hand through his hair as he looked at her. It was thick, dark, wayward, a bit long, her scientist's brain logged automatically, then moved on to his clothes. White shirt, tight faded jeans, jacket casual, but expensively cut. Cashmere?

What was it Mandy had said? Don't be deceived by the jeans and the boyish grins. He's the premier new director in this country, and coming up fast to be one of the best in the world. He's good, and he knows it, and he's absolutely ruthless about getting where he wants to go.

She felt herself tremble under his hard scrutiny, certain he must see the deception at any moment. But he didn't.

'Mandy,' he said, and she noticed again how dark and liquid his voice was. 'Thank you for taking the time to come in.'

'You wanted to see me?'

What a daft thing to say. Of course he did, that was why she was here. Bella sat down and crossed her legs nervously, and his eyes followed the movement, noting the slender length of her limbs.

'I did.' He slid down into his chair and extended his legs casually, still scrutinising her. She felt uncomfortable. In her world, people did not stare at other people as if they were nothing more than lumps of meat on a butcher's slab. She recrossed her legs.

Another phone began to squawk and he cursed,

picked it up and dropped it back on the receiver to stop its ringing. 'My assistant, Caroline, has already left for Mauritius,' he said, 'and my secretary's gone to the dentist.'

She waited, her discomfort mounting by the minute.

'Look,' he said, 'I wanted a brief word with you, as it seems forever since we did the casting for this film. You must know about all the problems we've had with it? The main American backers pulled out at the last minute, and then there were problems getting to shoot in the Seychelles and we had to switch locations to Mauritius—sometimes it's seemed as if the whole project has been cursed from the start.'

She nodded. 'My agent told me.' Her agent. She had never had an agent in her life. It was amazing how smoothly the lie slipped out.

'We had to stitch a whole new deal together. It was pretty complicated. That's what held everything up all these months. But that's history now, thank heaven. I'm off to Mauritius tomorrow. Shooting starts in four days. You come out next week. If we stick to the schedule you'll be on the island for a week . . .'

Bella frowned. All this had been arranged for a long time. Mandy already had her instructions. She could not see the point of going over it now.

He saw her look at once. His eyes were extraordinary, she thought. They were a dark smoky grey, yet they were also light and penetrating, as if they were illuminated from behind by some inner light. They were night eyes, she thought irrelevantly, lit by silver moonlight.

'Look,' he said again, opening his hands on the desk for emphasis, 'you'll be joining the set when shooting's already been under way for a week. All the big stars will be there. Or rather, if things go to plan,

Dawn Spencer will have finished her scenes and left, but Guy de Vere will obviously be there and for a newcomer this sort of thing can be pretty overpowering. You've never acted with anyone in de Vere's league before, have you?'

She shook her head.

'That's what I thought. What I don't want is for you to feel overwhelmed. And neither do I want you to think that yours is just a small part, not very important, only ten minutes' screen time in the Mauritian scenes. You see, Mandy,' he gave her a look like a laser beam, 'the more I think about this picture, the more I realise the whole story turns around you and the qualities you can project into your part.'

Bella swallowed, almost hypnotised by his compelling eyes and voice.

'You see,' he tapped the dog-eared, coffee-stained script in front of him, 'unless people really believe that Grayson, whose whole life has become a wreck, whose wife has divorced him and whose job is in jeopardy because he's been drinking so much, who's lost almost everything including his self-respect, can get himself back on the road to salvation just because of a brief holiday affair with you . . . unless you can project that something, that, that——' his hands shaped a solid mass on the desk in front of him as he searched for words '——that elusive inner sensuality, that haunting freedom of youth, that purity, that Grayson sees, and knows he has never had, and wants so desperately—then the whole story fails to make sense. It becomes just another story of a cop on the tail of a drugs ring, with a bit of love interest and a big chase at the end.' His voice twisted, making clear just how much he would hate to make such a film.

'I see.' It seemed an inadequate response, just as she

felt entirely inadequate, an edgy figure sitting tensely on her chair, compared to the character he had just described. If only Mandy were here to hear all this, she thought longingly. She would be radiant with joy. She had known the part was important—'It's my big break, Bell,' she had insisted, 'the one I've waited for all these years'—but to hear it from the boss himself would have made her flower with triumph.

His eyes suddenly narrowed, as he scrutinised her taut figure. 'Have you lost weight?'

'No.' She tensed harder in her seat, sensing danger.

'You look different. There's a different quality to you.'

The scrutiny went on and on. His eyes weren't lit by moonlight, she realised suddenly, but by the power of his high-octane thoughts. Her face must have registered her dismay because he instantly put up a hand. 'Don't look like that. You look fine, absolutely fine. Better, actually. Whatever it is, I like it. I just wondered what it was.'

'Maybe it's the hair? It's shorter.'

'Maybe.' His eyes looked sceptical, but he snapped back to the matter in hand. 'What this is, Mandy, is a pep talk. As simple as that. I want you to fly out next week in the right frame of mind. Absolutely psyched up to the hilt to make this your best performance ever.'

'I'll certainly try.' Her voice sounded thin and high, unconvincing even to her own ears. This was hopeless. For Mandy's sake, she had to try harder than this. 'I'm glad you told me,' she continued more steadily. 'I knew it was a key part, but it's useful to know how you see it. It'll help me to work on it.' She hoped and prayed she had chosen the right kind of phrases. She knew nothing about film jargon.

He was leaning back in his chair now, elbows linked

behind his head, a casual pose but with a gaze like razors and a doubtful set to his eyes. She wasn't convincing him, she could see that. She had to try harder. There would be no point in her being here like this, trying to pass herself off as Mandy, if the only outcome of the meeting was that Mandy got the sack.

She mentally gritted her teeth, while her brain whirled anxiously through all the instructions Mandy had heaped upon her. What was the last thing she had said?

'Relax, Bella, really throw yourself into it. Enjoy being someone else for an hour. Even flirt, if you feel it would help. Flounce and pout. I would. After all, I'm in the film to be sexy, and he'd probably love it—he's a notorious womaniser.'

In vain she had protested that she had never flounced or pouted in her life, but her iron-hearted sister had just laughed and said pointedly that she was far too uptight, and it was about time she tried.

'It's what actresses do.'

'Mandy, I'm *not* an actress!'

'You are. For a day. Anyway, with your looks it's a crime not to.'

Now she looked at Luke Retford's hard, doubtful gaze and knew she had to act as she had never acted in her life. Because behind those compelling eyes was a brain turning fast, and she guessed that what it was thinking was whether or not he had made a big mistake casting Mandy Latham in this part, and whether or not it was too late to find an alternative actress to fit the bill.

She flicked her eyes from his and confronted her own reflection in a mirror on the far wall. It startled her. The girl in the mirror was not the pretty, quietly dressed reflection that usually met her eyes, but a stunning blonde, with a tumbling mane of sun-streaked hair. Make-up darkened her violet eyes to dusky pools, and her wide, sensuous mouth was highlighted with red. Her slim body, in a black shirt dress, undone low at the neck and with the collar and cuffs turned up, looked both sexy and crisply professional at the same time.

She could see it was a stunning combination that worked superbly, and made her look every inch the hot young film actress she was meant to be, and it gave her such a rush of confidence that, on the strength of it, she managed to glide her eyes back to Luke Retford and let her lips loosen into a sexy pout.

'I won't let you down,' she murmured, and was astonished to find that her voice came out differently, low and languorous.

The effect was instantaneous. She could see Luke begin to relax before her very eyes, as he saw again those qualities he had cast her for. What next? She thought of Mandy, and how she used her eyes, and allowed her own lashes to drop in dark fans over her high cheekbones before looking up at Luke again with a warm look. His own eyes warmed instantly in response. She wanted to laugh at the heady power she was beginning to discover. Slowly she recrossed her legs, allowing the sheer black nylon to rasp seductively. Luke's eyes followed the movement, and she saw the muscles of his throat move as he swallowed.

It was amazing. With just a few tricks and gestures she had transformed herself into a siren and roused a clear desire in this tough, sophisticated man. She held his eyes, batting her eyelids slowly, and he gave her a long look that held obvious appreciation.

'Do you have any problems with the part?' His

voice had changed a little, too, and was roughened.

She slanted her gaze back at him. It was getting easier by the minute. Without thinking, she allowed her tongue to moisten her lips before she spoke, a seductive glimpse of pink. 'There *are* one or two things, but they are only minor. I'd rather leave it until we're filming.' Apart from anything else, she did not know what they were. Mandy had said she was worried about some of the lines, but she hadn't gone into detail.

'OK. That suits me. I find people tend to forget things if they go over them too early.'

Bella smiled lusciously at him, but her brain registered the remark coldly. You mean you think most actresses are bimbos, without a brain in their heads, she thought cynically, and then lowered her heavy lashes hastily, in case any hint of scepticism crept into her gaze.

'However, I'd like to run over a few thoughts I've had, just to give you something to chew on on that long flight out.'

She raised her eyes and watched him sit up and cross his forearms on the desk, regarding her darkly. 'Remember, Dee Purvis is a young girl, just eighteen, never been abroad before,' he rattled out. 'She's won this exotic holiday through a competition in a magazine—if it weren't for that, she would probably never have ventured further afield than a package holiday to Spain. Her boyfriend was supposed to come with her, but they split up just before the holiday. Deciding to go ahead on her own was probably the biggest decision of her life so far, but a vital one. I see her as a girl just teetering on the edge of life, beginning to realise how big the pool can be. She's also teetering on the edge of her own womanhood, finding out her own powers to captivate men . . .'

She flushed as his eyes flickered across her face. It was almost as if he knew the new games she had been playing. But she managed to hold his gaze without guiltily looking away.

'She's naïve,' he continued, 'and fairly innocent, although not stupid. She's been to bed with her boyfriend, but that doesn't mean she knows what sex is about. She certainly doesn't know anything about love, and nothing at all about suffering and pain. Grayson falls for her looks first, and then her touching vulnerability. But what really gets to him, I think, is her bedrock honesty and common sense. If she sees a spade, it doesn't even cross her mind to call it anything else. Remember, as a cop, he's spent all his life dealing with frauds and criminals, and he's come to feel that he himself is tainted by all that, as grubby as they are. Now Dee comes along and not only makes him feel young again, but also somehow fresh—as if he could start all over again and make his life come out differently.

'Which, of course, is what he tries to do—and, although he can't do anything about the past, he does manage to shape a better future for himself. Not that you have to worry about the details of that at this stage since you don't come back into the proceedings again until the last scene. After the first twenty minutes you're not on screen again until the very end.'

'But surely, if it's because of Dee that he feels life is worth living again, wouldn't he try and find her the minute she's back in England?' she said, her logical brain seeing an instant flaw in the story.

'No. He's old enough and wise enough to realise that there's no future for them together, that it was enough just to have known her. At least he is at first, until his need to see her again overrides all his saner instincts.'

'And then it's a disaster?'

'More or less—haven't you read the script?' Luke's voice sharpened.

'Oh, yes. But my agent said you might have changed the end,' she improvised hastily.

'Mmm. It's true I haven't finalised the shape of that last scene. But there's clearly no way they can walk off into the sunrise together.'

She regarded him steadily, musing on what a strange world film-making must be, forever dealing with the fictional emotions of make-believe characters. Nothing could be further from her world of hard figures and solid facts.

'What I want you to work on, Mandy, is that crucial mixture of innocence and sensuality, vulnerability and good sense, that so completely knocks Grayson off his feet. Can you do that for me?'

Bella came back to the moment, remembering her role, and flapped her eyelids slowly once or twice. 'Yes, I'll work on it.' Her voice was husky again.

'Good.' At his elbow a phone shrilled. He picked it up. 'Retford.'

She watched him as he riffled through papers on his desk as he talked. His forearm was tanned and shaded with dark hair and she could see the bones and muscles working together under the skin. His fingers, as he scribbled a note, fascinated her, as did the line of his shoulder where he hunched the phone to his ear, and the wayward dark hair that curled over his collar. His profile was near perfect, she thought, with its straight nose and sensual lips and stubborn chin, but it was his eyes that made him so extraordinarily compelling, eyes that seemed to change colour by the minute, from a penetrating blue to darkest grey, as his thoughts and emotions changed.

As she stared at him he glanced across at her, and she remembered hastily to change her lips to a pout and her eyes to a smoulder. After a moment she shook back her hair from her face in a movement which allowed her full figure to strain briefly against the cotton of her dress.

His eyes darkened to navy and he gave her a long look from under his lids, filled with such open sensuality that it made her pulses race. And as he finished his conversation with an abrupt, 'Yes, yes. OK, then, do it,' he did not take his eyes from hers.

As he replaced the receiver, the look continued. 'OK, Mandy,' he said finally, and he smiled slowly, showing white teeth that made her think of biting kisses. He got up from behind his desk and came round to lift her to her feet with a hand at her elbow. Where his fingers touched her bare skin she wanted to shiver. Then he took her hand, still looking deep into her eyes. 'I'm looking forward to working with you in Mauritius,' he said seductively. 'Very much looking forward to it.'

'So am I,' Bella breathed back at him, and looked up from under her lashes into his extraordinary eyes.

'I think you'll be terrific,' he said, not letting go of her hand. 'Absolutely terrific.'

She was mesmerised by him, a mouse transfixed by a hunting cat. 'I hope so. I'm certainly looking forward to working with you.'

'Let's hope we get a little time to get to know each other—socially.'

'That would be very nice,' she breathed, and her lips trembled and parted at his nearness.

'I hear Mauritius is a very romantic island,' he continued.

She tossed her hair gently. 'I can hardly wait to see it," she murmured.

'All those deserted beaches and moonlit nights . . .'

'Mmm—it sounds wonderful.'

'I'm sure it will be wonderful.' His voice was a low, dark rasp. 'There's just one thing, one tiny little thing . . .' he continued silkily.

'I'm at your command,' she murmured back, before a cold ripple of apprehension went through her, as she saw his gaze grow black and harsh. Too late she realised that she had been led into a trap. She had not been the one playing games with him. He had, with her. What a fool she was. Only someone as naïve and innocent as she could have thought a little bit of blatant flirting would have had a man like Luke on his knees.

His voice, when he spoke, was harsh with authority. 'It's this. You might be a terrific little seductress, Mandy. You certainly like using your eyes and mouth and all those other bits God gave you, but just remember it's your acting skills I'm hiring, not your flirting ones. If I see any hint of that clichéd pin-up-girl act in my movie, even the merest glimpse, then you'll be looking for new work faster than you can run your tongue over that slippery lip gloss of yours. By the time I see you next, I want you thinking Dee Purvis, looking Dee Purvis, being Dee Purvis!' I'm sorry to disappoint you, but it's her I'm interested in, and only her, no matter how alluring the charms of Mandy Latham herself might be. And I expect you to remember that every single day you're working for me. Got it?'

He raked her furiously blushing face.

'Yes,' was all she could get out.

'Good. Then I'll see you in Mauritius.'

He opened the door and she fled down the stairs.

Oh, no, you won't, she thought thankfully as she went. Oh, no, you won't!

CHAPTER TWO

BELLA sat in a café two streets away until her legs had stopped trembling and the scarlet blush of shame that had flared across her cheeks at Luke's contemptuous words had subsided.

To still her churning, embarrassed thoughts she fished a copy of the *New Scientist* out of her bag and tried to concentrate on an article on new drugs for heart patients, but it was hopeless. Time after time the print swam in front of her eyes and reformed itself into Luke's scornful eyes and when she looked up she caught the café owner's curious stare as he looked in puzzlement from the low cleavage of her black dress to the heavyweight literature in her hand.

Well, let him stare, she thought with angry misery. She knew she looked incongruous—she *was* incongruous. She should never have tried flirting, especially with a man like Luke, when she was so completely unpractised. After all, most of her efforts over the past few years had been spent trying to persuade her male colleagues to look beyond the startling beauty of her huge purple eyes, and the curve of her generous mouth, in favour of the seriousness of her work.

She pulled a face. She ought to go home and tell Mandy that their deception had worked, that Luke had been taken in, but she balked at having to go over the whole excruciating episode so soon, so instead she turned eastward and made for the university library where she immersed herself for two blissful hours in the quiet absorption of catching up on the latest scientific papers in her particular corner of the vast field that was modern medical research.

'Well?' Mandy knelt up eagerly in bed as she slammed the door of the flat behind her. 'You were ages. Was it all right? Did we get away with it?'

'We did.'

Bella smiled grimly at her twin sister, younger than her by half an hour, and sank tiredly down at the dressing-table, glancing at her vivid reflection. 'Ugh, Mandy, I don't know how you can bear to wear all this make-up all the time. It feels like mud.'

With relief she began to clean it away, seeing her own face reappear again. She and Mandy were identical, but at twenty-four, and pursuing quite different careers, they had come to present themselves to the world so differently that it was rare these days for them to be mistaken for each other.

'A tool of the trade, and it's not all the time, anyway,' said Mandy impatiently. 'But what about Luke Retford? Did he think you were me?'

'Yes. He asked me if I'd lost weight—he said I looked different—but I lied and said it was my hair.' She recounted the interview, watching her sister's eyes glow like coals as she told her what he had said about her part.

'Oh, it's my big break! I know it is! I can just feel it in my bones. Tell me again what he said . . .'

Bella told her, thinking how beautiful her extrovert and theatrical sister looked sitting cross-legged, in pyjamas, among her rumpled sheets. Luke Retford's eyes would certainly darken if he could see this sight, she thought, and for some reason a bitter stab of irritation went through her. But when Mandy tossed her hair back a livid red patch showed on her cheek.

Mandy saw where her sister's eyes went, and put up her hand to finger the patch. 'It's smaller today, isn't it, Bell?' she quizzed her anxiously. 'I'm sure it is. And I don't feel quite so grotty. I'm sure it's just a horrid boil that's giving me a bit of a fever. There'll be no trace of it in a week's time. But I would have just hated Retford to see me like this. He would have off-loaded me on the spot.'

Bella thought about Luke's ruthless eyes, and thought Mandy was probably right. She also thought the infection looked, if anything, worse. 'I don't know. I think you should call the doctor, just to be sure—you might be able to get some ointment that'll clear it up quicker.'

'I will, tomorrow. Now that I know everything's OK. Oh, Bell, you're the best sister anyone could ever have. I'll never forget what you've done.' And she jumped up and embraced her in a bear-like hug.

'Hey, hey. Don't be too grateful.' Laughing, Bella extricated herself. 'You haven't heard everything yet. I tried to do what you told me. I pouted and flirted like mad, and I thought I was doing wonderfully. I was certainly getting a reaction, but just as I was going——' she blushed fiercely at the memory '—I got told in no uncertain terms that he didn't go for such cheap tricks, that I'd have to stop flirting and start acting when I arrived on set or I'd be out on my ear!'

Mandy just laughed. 'If that's the only negative thing he said to you, you must have done fine. He's got a terrible reputation, really terrible. He's the tough guy of the British film industry. Everyone who ever works with him swears they'll never do it again. Then they do, because he's so good, and gets such brilliant work out of everyone. They say he could get a kitchen table to turn in a star performance if he had to. Phew.' She climbed on to her bed again and lay back among the pillows, looking pale and tired.

'Are you all right?'

'Mm. Just a bit whacked. What did you think of him? He's quite something, isn't he?'

'Mm. Quite.' Bella suddenly saw again that dark, lidded stare and felt her body suffuse with heat. She looked away, not wanting Mandy to guess at her feelings. 'What do you know about him?'

'Only what everyone knows. He started out in television documentaries, then did commercials to raise enough money to set up his own production company. He made *Night-run*, and *Decline of the Empire*——'

'What?'

'Oh, Bell, where've you been hiding all these years? They each won a fistful of awards. He was deluged with offers from Hollywood, but he always said he would carry on working here.'

'Not everyone follows the fortunes of the film industry as closely as you.'

'They don't have to. Luke Retford's a household name.'

'Not in this household. At least, not in my half of it!'

'Well, you barely ever lift your head from your books, do you? Hey, what's eating you?' Mandy's eyes flicked shrewdly over her. 'Don't tell me you fancy him.'

Bella turned fiercely, the full stress of the day finally taking its toll, and her words ripped off her tongue like torn silk. 'No, Mandy, I don't, as you so crudely put it, fancy him! I don't fancy any man who looks at women as though they were specimens on a shop shelf! Neither do I have much time for arrogant men who talk to women as if they've scarcely got a brain in their head. He's a good-looking man, I don't deny it, but he's about as much my type as an all-in mud wrestler, and I'm absolutely delighted to think that after today I need never see him again!'

Mandy slid slowly down beneath the covers until only the top of her head was visible, and waited for the length of a dramatic pause.

'Oh,' she said finally, her voice muffled by sheets, 'so you *do* fancy him.' Then she pulled the sheets up high as a hairbrush came whizzing angrily through the air towards her.

Bella didn't fancy Luke Retford, of course she didn't. But as she bathed and went to bed that night his face and figure danced tormentingly before her eyes, and during the night her dreams were haunted by dark eyes and a deep liquid voice that made her quiver inside.

'Hey, Bella, you look different,' said Pete Rawlins, her co-researcher, when she walked into the cramped broom cupboard they shared as an office in the Institute of Health the next morning. He peered myopically up at her over his glasses and gave a loud wolf whistle. 'The institute won't know what's hit it.'

'It's only my hair,' she said shortly. 'I had it layered.'

'Well, it's better than that kind of bun thing you used to have,' said Pete, absent-mindedly scratching his stomach where his shirt had parted from his trousers. 'Have you seen Roger this morning?'

'No, why?' her voice was sharp with irritation. Why was it that the very sight of Pete, with whom she had worked perfectly amiably for the past year, set her teeth on edge? Why did his mousy beard irritate her, and his pullover and his pale, cheerful eyes? She knew why, and she cursed Luke Retford silently under her breath.

'He says the computer's down again. We won't be able to process those figures from the Scottish survey until Thursday at the earliest.'

'Hell and damnation! Does nothing in this place work properly?'

'No. I'm surprised you're even surprised any more.' Pete looked at her. 'You certainly got out of bed the wrong side this morning.'

'There is only one side. The other's against the wall,' Bella snapped.

She sat at her desk and seethed for a while. 'I think I'll go down to the lab and see Sue about next month's conference. She said she'd read our paper over for us.'

'There's no point. She's already left for Greece. Term's finished, don't forget, in fact I get the feeling we're the only two people left in the entire building, and I'm off tomorrow. A whole summer in the States—I can't wait.'

'I wish you could. Wait. At least until after the conference. You're much better than me at speaking in public——'

'Nonsense. That's a typically female lack of self-confidence. It's mainly your work, and you'll do it just fine. Sue's left you a few comments——they're on your desk.'

Bella picked them up and read them, frowning. 'She's right. We haven't explained the basis of the sample fully enough. I'll have to rewrite the whole blasted section.'

'Language!'

'Well, *you* don't have to do it!'

'And neither do you. It's an hour's work at the most on the word processor. What's all the fuss?'

She sat down gloomily. 'You're right. I'm just looking for something to hang my bad mood on.'

'What you need is a holiday. What are your plans for the summer?'

'No plans,' she said lightly, but her heart sank. Normally she and Mandy took off somewhere together, but this year all Mandy could think about was her film part, and her forthcoming trip to Mauritius.

Once again Luke Retford's face came infuriatingly to mind. How would he and Mandy get on together in Mauritius? she wondered. Mandy was a natural flirt, and Luke had shown her how willingly he could respond to that, if he had half a mind. Would the inevitable happen? Would they have a brief, tempestuous fling among the white beaches and whispering palms? She did not pry too closely into Mandy's private life, but she knew enough to know it was considerably more relaxed than her own. Jealousy stabbed through her like a knife, making her shut her eyes with pain. For the first time ever in her life, she envied her sister.

'I'm going, Pete!' She banged a pile of files together and stood up. 'It's far too nice a day to waste time here. I'm going home to work in the garden.'

She almost ran out of the gloomy room and down the dully painted, echoing corridors, frustration snapping at her heels. A few male colleagues greeted her, most of them as mild-mannered and unremarkable as Pete, and she smiled woodenly back at them, but today the very sight of them irritated her unbearably. Out in the sunlight she ran down the steps as if demons were behind her, and jumped on to a passing red bus.

She climbed upstairs and sat watching the familiar city streets pass by as the bus laboured through Bloomsbury and turned into Oxford Street.

Suddenly she saw the road she had walked down yesterday, to reach Luke's office, and before she had realised what she was doing she had whirled down the steps and stood panting on the pavement.

Her reflection looked back at her from a shop window, light years away from the seductive, sultry actress of yesterday. Today she wore jeans, a white shirt and white loafers, with a denim jacket swinging casually from her shoulders. Her face was free of make-up and looked youthfully beautiful, and only the shaggy, layered hair remained as a reminder of the vamp she had been. Rummaging in her bag, she found an elastic band and scooped as much hair as she could manage into a pony-tail so that the transformation was complete.

Slowly she walked down the bustling streets of Soho. The sleazy strip clubs were beginning to give way to smart new designer offices, she noticed. Fresh coffee perfumed the air, and she could hear the distant cries of a street market.

This was Luke's world, she thought. A world full of contrasts and chaos and life. It could be a different city from the orderly, tree-lined streets around the university. It was the difference between their lives, really. He dealt with the shifting vagaries of fantasy and fiction, while she, as a medical statistician, only dealt with rigorously checked facts.

And this was his office. She stood, looking at the discreet plaque by the anonymous door, and remembered her terror of yesterday. No one in the world would have got her to pull such a stunt except Mandy, but then Mandy, she reflected honestly, could probably get her to do anything. She loved her younger twin as she loved herself, and sometimes almost more

'What the hell——?'

'Oh, my goodness!'

As she'd loitered by the door it had suddenly been flung open and Luke had come out, at a lope, his hand already out to hail a passing black cab. He hadn't expected a stationary figure to be blocking his way, and he had jolted her shoulder so hard as he'd hastened past that the collision had sent his papers flying.

'I'm sorry——' Her immediate reaction was an instinctive apology, even though she had done nothing wrong. She turned to help pick up the scattered documents. Then, as she saw the lean profile of his face, angry and impatient, she began to tremble. He was already bending this way and that, retrieving the files. He looked up, back at the taxi to make sure it was waiting, then at her.

As he did so, as their eyes met for the first time, something quite extraordinary happened to his face. He had glanced in her direction with unconcealed irritation, but then his expression changed. His smoky eyes darkened. He frowned. She could see puzzlement and astonishment in his look, fighting with blatant disbelief. He was a man seeing a ghost, something that just could not be, and he could not tear his eyes from her.

And something was happening to her, too. At his intense look, she felt warmth spread through her, darkening her eyes to huge pools of purple and softening her mouth. Her heart was racing. Any minute now, she could see, he would speak, delay her with a hand on her arm—— Abruptly she dropped the papers she had picked up back on to the pavement, turned swiftly and sped away into the crowds thronging Shaftesbury Avenue. And the moment was gone, leaving nothing except the thundering of her heart that did not still until she reached home.

Back at the flat, though, there were more problems.

'Look!' cried Mandy in anguish. 'Isn't it awful? Oh, Bell, what am I going to do?' Mandy had been asleep when Bella had left this morning, but now she saw that overnight several more unsightly blotches had appeared on Mandy's face. 'They're in my hair, too. They itch, it's agony.'

'It looks like chicken-pox,' Bella said with a crisp matter-of-factness that hid her distress for her sister. 'You'd better stay in bed. I'll get the doctor.'

'I've already called him, he's coming over.' Mandy flopped back. 'It's hopeless,' she said in a flat voice. 'I'll never be able to do the part in this state. It'll be weeks before I look normal again.'

The doctor confirmed chicken-pox at a glance, and also confirmed Mandy's gloomy diagnosis. The scars might take weeks to fade, he said. Although, if she did not scratch them, they should leave no permanent damage.

'Chicken-pox,' said Mandy, with disgust. 'After all these years, all those seasons playing pantomime in Preston and Paignton, all those fruitless auditions, all those recalls—then I finally get it, the film part I've waited years for, and what happens? I get chicken-pox!'

Bella had never heard her so bitter, and it wrung her heart.

'I might as well throw in the towel. I'll never get another chance like this.'

'You might. You could ring up Luke Retford and explain, and ask him to bear you in mind for the future. He obviously thinks a lot of you.'

Mandy gave her a withering glance.

'It doesn't work like that. Oh, yes, he likes me. He likes me for *this* movie, not for any others. There are a million actresses out there, Bella. All hungry. Half of them beautiful—no, it's finished.'

Gloom hung heavy in the small bedroom, while Bella's practical mind turned the problem over and over.

'How much do you appear on screen in Mauritius?'

'Not a lot, and only two scenes where I have to speak. That's the awful irony. My main scene comes right at the end, when Grayson finally confronts me in Wales. And that's right at the end of the schedule. I'll probably be as right as rain by then, but what use will that be?'

'Oh, Mandy.' Bella reached out and squeezed her sister's hand.

Mandy pulled it away. 'Unclean, unclean!' she tolled, savagely.

'Well, if I'm going to catch it, I'm going to catch it.' Bella sighed, her own violet eyes scanning her sister's identical deep purple gaze. 'Oh, love. I'm so sorry.'

'Yes, well.' Mandy shut her eyes. 'It's my own silly fault for getting into such a precarious profession. I should have done something nice and solid, like you.'

'Nice and boring, you mean. I can hardly see you bent over a computer all day.'

'No, I've never shared your views on the romance of figures. Give me flesh and blood any day. Preferably Luke Retford's flesh and blood. Preferably offering a nice fat script. Oh——' Sobs choked her words.

Bella shut her eyes tight against the images Mandy's words roused in her mind—a lean, restless body, and grey, brooding eyes. That strange, complex look that had gone between them that morning.

'If I could do anything, I would,' she said, painfully, 'you know that.'

'You could make that call,' Mandy replied dully. 'You know, the one that pulls the plug on me. I don't think I could bear it.' She closed her eyes again and, as Bella watched, a tear squeezed out from under her exquisitive dark lashes and rolled down her cheek, stopping only at the obstruction of one of her spots. The sight made Bella want to howl in sympathy.

Instead she stole away and picked up the telephone.

'Mr Retford is out for the rest of the day,' said a woman's voice. 'Can I take a message?'

'No.' She put the receiver down. The band in her hair was pulling, making her head ache. She took it out and, shaking out her newly shaggy locks, went back into Mandy's room.

'Surely they could do something with make-up?' she burst out. She could not bear the weight of her sister's wretchedness. 'I mean, they paint spots *on* people, surely they can paint them off? You could at least ask.'

Mandy opened her eyes, and as she looked at her sister her eyes suddenly sharpened. 'Bella, you look just like me!'

'Of course I do. That was the whole point of this haircut.'

'I bet if we wore the same clothes even Mum would have a job to know who was who.'

'She'd look for the scar.' Bella's fingers went to the thin white line that marked her collarbone, the relic of a childhood fall into savage brambles.

'It hardly shows—to people who don't know to look for it.' Mandy's gaze was purposeful now. Bella saw it. She blinked twice. She couldn't possibly be thinking——? She was.

'Oh, no. No! No way.' Bella put up a hand to ward off the unspoken suggestion. 'I'm no actress.'

'You were yesterday.'

'Yesterday was one thing. It was only for ten minutes.'

'But, Bella, just think. That was ten whole minutes

under the scrutiny of the big man himself. And he didn't notice anything, did he? That's the ultimate test. On set it would be different. There would be hundreds of people milling around. No one would pay you much attention.'

'Oh, no? Only when I had to go out under the lights and actually speak your lines—they'd notice then, all right.'

'You could do it as well as me, easily. Probably better. It was always you who got the lead parts at school, remember? The only difference between us is that I *wanted* to be an actress, you didn't.' Mandy was warming to the idea by the minute.

'No, Mandy. The answer's no.'

'You could. You told me you had no commitments, now that term's practically finished.'

'I could. But I'm not going to.'

'You might even enjoy it. Just think—a week on a tropical island, snorkelling along the coral reef, dining under the palm trees. It'll be fun, Bella, a real change for you——'

'From my dull life, you mean? Thank you, but I like my life.'

'I know you do. But, let's face it, it's hardly exotic, is it? Lecturing first-year students on regional differences in breast cancer and lung disease. Then spending hours in that poky little cubby-hole peering at a computer screen.'

A mixture of dreadful fear and crazy longing made Bella angry. 'Well, I don't see what's so damn exotic about sitting at home waiting for your agent to ring, or taking waitressing jobs to make ends meet. That's exactly why I'd never be an actress if you paid me!'

'You don't have to be an actress. Only pretend to be one for a week. Don't let's fight, Bella. I don't

think your life's a bit dull. I know you're doing what
you enjoy. I just think that sometimes you could do
with a bit of fun in your life, a bit more enjoyment.
Ever since you finished with Nick, you've done
nothing but work. It's not natural——'

'Neither is pretending to be someone else all the
time.' But Bella was mollified. She knew Mandy
cared for her in the same close way she cared for
Mandy. 'Just look at it from my point of view,' she
pleaded. 'They'd all be talking about—I don't
know—booms and grips and gaffs and things—and
I wouldn't understand a word they were saying. And
suppose they asked me about my previous jobs, or
people I was supposed to know?'

'Then you could tell them. You know exactly what
I've been doing—and I could always give you some
crib notes.'

'I'd stick out like a sore thumb.'

'No, you wouldn't. You could be friendly, but quiet.
Do what people tell you, and come home. Film people
all have egos like houses. They'd be far too busy
listening to the sound of their own voices to worry
about not hearing yours.'

Bella looked at her sister's desperate eyes.

'Oh, Bella, you could just sneak off on your own
most of the time. You could spend ninety per cent of
the time sunbathing and reading a good book.'

'And what about the other ten per cent?'

'Put yourself in the expert's hands. I could tutor you
before you go, then all you have to do is whatever Luke
tells you. I've told you, he can coax a performance out
of a table leg.'

The force of her sister's need seemed to scorch Bella's
skin, and so did something else: an image of Luke,
bronzed, shirtless, on a tropical beach. And a need to be

near him took hold of her like fire. She swayed, appalled at the strength of these feelings that had come out of the blue to bend and blur her judgement.

'Please, Bella. You could do it, I just know you could. You could be my stand-in for this first bit of filming, then I'd still be able to do the main scene myself.'

Bella felt herself pulled this way and that by emotions that surged through her like running tides. She took a deep breath.

'I'm sorry, Mandy. I'd do almost anything for you, you know that. But I won't do this. We'd never get away with it. Do you understand? I can't do it, and I won't.'

CHAPTER THREE

BELLA thought she was going to pass out. The sun blazed on her neck and painted dizzy blackness in front of her eyes.

Guy de Vere—the legendary sex symbol—stood before her. He was shorter and older than she had imagined and the heavy screen make-up sat on his face like an orange mask. She thought she might burst into hysterical giggles, or faint dead away on the burning sand. She knew she would not be sick because her stomach had already rejected its breakfast and lunch, back in the privacy of her hotel bathroom.

'OK. Go.' Luke's deep, authoritative voice cut through her humming dizziness. There was the bang of a clapperboard. This was the moment she had been dreading ever since she'd arrived on the island two days ago. Now it was here and it was a thousand million times worse than the worst of her fears.

There were people everywhere, a huge blurred circle of pale oval faces, all turned towards her. Ahead of her she could see Guy de Vere stepping nearer to her. She could see his mouth moving, speaking the lines she had read and reread until she knew every letter of them by heart, but she was wooden, a statue rooted to the spot. She looked in despair at Guy, and panic pounded in her breast. Any moment she would have to speak and her tongue was the size of a melon in her mouth. She broke into a cold sweat.

'Cut!'

Luke's voice came from somewhere behind her. She had scarcely seen him since she had arrived in

Mauritius until he had briefed her for the scene just a few minutes ago, and now he was only a disembodied voice, like God, somewhere far off.

She turned. He signalled a make-up girl forward, who carefully dabbed the beads of perspiration from her forehead.

'OK.' The clapperboard banged again.

It was back into the nightmare. Guy de Vere advanced again, spoke again, the cameras whirred. They were on the beach. Dazzling white sand spread away in all directions. The heat was unbelievable.

'Cut!'

Luke's voice, angry, carried across all the people. 'Mandy, for heaven's sake, what is this? You're just standing there like a lump of stone. Get to work—that's what you're here for.'

Everyone was staring at Bella. She shook her head. A hundred wasps seemed to be buzzing in her ears, and tears came into her eyes.

'Again,' Luke said, and the clapperboard clapped and her nightmore repeated itself. Only this time it was worse. Everything seemed unreal, and the buzzing in her ears drowned out all other sound. She felt herself swaying.

'Cut!'

Luke came towards her, clearly furious. Guy de Vere put up a warning hand to him. From close up he could obviously see her distress. 'Give her a break. She just needs a bit of time, a bit of encouragement to get going——'

'I'll give her all the encouragement in the world when she deigns to put herself at first base,' Luke seethed. 'What is this, Mandy? What the hell do you think you're doing?'

Bella saw his eyes scowling down at her and put a

hand to her temples, fighting back tears. The urge to confess the whole impossible deception to him was almost overwhelming. She bit hard on her lips.

'Hey, take it easy.' Guy's voice was warm, in contrast to Luke's cold fury, and she clutched at his kindness like a drowning man at a straw. His blue eyes were deep and concerned. He crinkled a smile down at her. 'It's always tough, this first take, especially when you haven't made a movie before.'

She nodded. 'It's so hot . . .' she got out, but the buzzing was worse and the white beach seemed to dance with black spots, and somewhere in the middle of it all was Luke's angry, contemptuous face. 'I think I'm going to faint,' she murmured, and then she did.

When she came round she was lying on her own bed with the cane blinds unrolled to shadow the blinding sun. A girl she had not seen before was sponging her wrists and temples with cool water.

'Mandy,' she said coolly, when she saw Bella's eyes open, 'are you all right? You've been out for ages. Luke told me to get a doctor if you didn't come round soon.'

'Yes.' She felt as limp as a rag doll, but otherwise well. She looked at the girl suspiciously.

'Who are you?'

'I'm Caroline, Luke's assistant.'

'Oh.' She shut her eyes again.

'He's not very pleased with you—as you can probably imagine.'

'Yes.' She swallowed. 'I made a complete fool of myself, didn't I?'

'So I gather.' Caroline dropped the sponge back into the bowl of water with disdainful fingers and got up to dry her hands. 'I wasn't on set when it happened. Luke called me over here later. But *if* it was the heat——' she seemed to lay a sceptical emphasis on the 'if' '—you surely know you should always wear a hat out of doors? It protects the top of your head.'

Bella squinted at her guardian with dislike. Caroline wore a cool white dress and had glossy black hair pulled back in a white ribbon, and her almond skin and even features looked as if they had never been sweaty and distraught in her life.

'How did I get here?' she found herself saying

Caroline turned down her mouth expressively. 'I gather Luke scooped you up and deposited you here. Then he left. You should think yourself lucky. He's in a fine old fury. Do you know what a wasted half-day costs him?'

'Oh . . .' Bella sighed heavily.

'He says the sun's too low to shoot again today.'

Bella levered herself up, trying to ignore the way her head started to thump as she moved. 'Maybe if I went out now, there'd be time——'

Caroline put a cold, restraining hand on her shoulder. 'No. You're to stay and rest. I'm to stay and make you. Those are his express orders, and he's not used to being disobeyed. Anyway, he's gone off with some of the crew to the other side of the island, to get some background shots.'

'Oh.' Bella sank back and closed her eyes. She felt exhausted and miserable, but calmer than before. The sheer terror of this afternoon must have been cathartic, because she had the certain knowledge, deep inside, that the worst had passed. She might not turn in a brilliant performance, but at least she felt that she could now go through the motions, and that if she opened her lips words would come out of them.

She must have slept, because when she opened her eyes later the blinds were rolled up and the room was awash with the last vivid reds of the tropical sunset. Where Caroline had been sitting, there was Luke, straddling the chair backwards, with his arms laid along the back of it and his eyes on her as if he had been watching her for a long time.

Her heart bumped with shock at the sight.

'Hello, Mandy,' His tone was curt with anger

Bella sat up quickly. 'I didn't know you were here! I'm so sorry for what happened this afternoon——' She was still wearing the bikini and beach robe that had been her costume for the scene, she realised, although Caroline, or someone, must have sponged her face free of heavy stage make-up.

'I still don't know what *did* happen.' His voice and eyes told her all she needed to know about his pent-up fury.

'I'm all right now. It must just have been the sun, it seemed so hot. And first-night nerves, or rather first-day nerves. It won't happen again, I promise.' She was gabbling from nerves, and he frowned dismissively.

'I sincerely hope it was the sun. I haven't any use for actresses who faint at the sight of a camera——'

'It wasn't that——'

'No?' He was harshly disbelieving. 'Well, let's hope so. Only you were looking so terrified as if you'd never seen a film set in your life before.'

'Well, I haven't! That is—I mean—I've only done television work, and that's different. Everything's on a much smaller scale.' The elaborate set of notes Mandy had given her about her background and work lay in the suitcase across the room. She wished she had X-ray eyes, to refresh her memory.

He shifted on his chair and she saw the strength of his thigh muscles straining against the white cotton of his trousers, and a strange stirring happened inside her. She had to look quickly away from him. There was a silence in the room. She looked back. He had sunk his chin on to his crossed forearms and was rubbing his thumb reflectively along his mouth as he scoured her with his gaze. His eyes were very dark, she noticed, thoughtful and grim. His lips—her gaze was drawn to them by the slight movement of his thumb—were strong and even.

To her horror, in the tense quiet that lay between them she suddenly felt her body tightening and lifting towards his male presence. She moved to pull her robe around her, but it was a futile gesture. His eyes had already shifted to the deep cleft of her breasts, and seen the way her flesh strained against the thin cotton of her brief bikini. He let his gaze linger there for a moment, as deliberate as a caress on her heated skin, and when he lifted his gaze to her eyes again there was a knowing warmth in his expression that had not been there before.

'So,' he said slowly, enigmatically, and he nodded slightly to himself as if confirming in his mind some private plan of action. Then he stretched his legs and stood up to pace the small room. When he spoke again his voice had lost its chill anger.

'I guess, Mandy, that I haven't taken into account just how green and inexperienced you are. I admit I half-expected you to be floundering out of your depth acting with Guy—that's one reason why I asked to see you in London before you flew out—but I didn't expect you to swoon away at the sight of three cameras and two sound booms.'

'And everyone else staring,' she put in. She remembered the nightmare circle of faces.

'Well, people do stare. You can't expect them to

hang about for hours, then look the other way when the action starts.' His voice harshened, but he checked his obvious impatience.

'No, I know, but——' She felt utterly foolish, and completely out of her depth. 'When you're feeling as though you're about to keel over with sunstroke, and there are all those blurred white faces at the edges of your vision—— 'She choked on an intake of breath and found to her horror it was becoming a sob. She swallowed fast, three times, feeling him watching her closely from across the shadowed room.

'Maybe you aren't up to it, Mandy!' he said abruptly. 'Maybe we should call it a day right here and now. I could get a replacement flown out in two days.'

'You can't do that!' She was aghast with horror. What would Mandy say?

'Of course I can. I can do anything I like. I'm God round here.' He stepped towards her, obviously meaning what he said.

'Nobody's God,' she countered defensively. 'You're under the same human rules as everyone else. You haven't got divine rights.'

'Maybe not, but I'm talking movies. And in movies I can raise people up to the heights, or vanquish them to the depths. I have done. Often. Why should you be an exception?'

'I've got my contract——'

'That's no problem. The lawyers could sort that out.'

'You haven't given me a chance yet——'

'You had the normal chance this afternoon. You blew it pretty thoroughly.'

'I was *ill*,' Bella protested vehemently. 'It was the heat and the people . . .'

He sat down on the edge of her bed, scrutinising her

face. 'You really want to do it? Really and truly? Only I got the distinct impression this afternoon that rather less than half your heart was in it.'

'I *do!*' She wasn't acting. She meant it. She was suddenly desperate to succeed at the task she had taken on, for her own dented pride as much as for Mandy's sake.

'Mmm.' He pushed a hand through his hair. 'Well, I'll give you one more try, but if you blow it again you're out. Do you understand? And you'd better get used to the crowds pretty fast. I've only ever shot one scene with just a skeleton crew—and that was under rather exceptional circumstances.'

'What was that?' she asked, as he clearly intended she should.

He grinned, showing white teeth against brown skin. There were fine fans of lines around the corners of his eyes, she noticed. She swallowed. When he spoke, his voice was low and teasing. 'I had a leading man and a leading lady who became, shall we say, very friendly during the course of making this particular movie. When it came to shooting the climactic love scene I'd seen enough of them together to suspect strongly that reality might overtake their acting skills when it came to the crunch—or should I say the clinch? So I backed my hunch, ordered everyone out, and shot the whole thing through in one take.'

'And . . . ?' She could not look away from him.

'And . . .' He paused, smiling deep into her eyes. 'It was a very good scene.'

'And were you right?'

He shrugged eloquently. 'Who's to say? They could just have been superlative actors.'

He laughed at the look on her face. 'You're shocked! There's no reason to be. Everyone was very happy. They with their performances, me with my movie—anyway, it's a tired old story now. It appeared on all the more scurrilous gossip pages at the time. I'm amazed you haven't heard it.'

She shook her head dumbly. 'Well, that certainly won't happen on this movie,' she said, thinking aloud as she remembered Guy's famously handsome but strangely unappealing face.

'No,' said Luke slowly, 'I somehow didn't think it would, not after seeing you and Guy together this afternoon. The more's the pity.' He reached out and took her hand, weighing her slender fingers lightly on his palm as his eyes lingered slowly over her hair, her figure, her bare legs, 'because that leaves the crucial question of what, exactly, it is we have to do to turn you on, Mandy Latham. To switch on that inner glow that I'm sure you have.'

Bella blushed under his scrutiny and for a moment there was silence. Surely he knew perfectly well what the answer to that was? she thought, as the blood in her veins leapt and tingled under his casual touch. Then she snatched her hand back and swung her legs down sharply from the bed.

'You don't have to do anything! I'll give you all the inner glow you want!' He was a despicable man, she decided, arrogant and rude and manipulative, and she longed for him to leave.

'On auto-pilot?' He raised a sceptical eyebrow.

'No! With my professional skills!'

Her anger plainly meant nothing to him at all. He levered himself casually from her bed. 'Well, let's hope they're all you clearly believe them to be, Mandy. But the proof of the pudding, as they say . . .'

Bella glanced at him quickly and saw the glint of his eyes in the rapidly deepening dusk and the bronzed skin of his forearms. The room was dark and intimate, and for a second her wayward imagination wondered what it would be like if he came over to her now, and touched her. Not casually, as he had taken her fingers on the bed, but as a man touched a woman he desired. But there was nothing further from his mind. All he was thinking about was his film, and how he could wring the best from this flawed performer.

'I admire your confidence,' he went on, 'but I have to say I don't share it. And I can't possibly risk a repeat performance of today, not at what it costs to run over schedule. So I've decided to rejig the shooting order, so you can do some of your non-speaking scenes first. When you've got over these first-night nerves, then we'll go for the big scenes.'

She nodded slowly, humiliated but secretly relieved as he went on, 'Tomorrow we'll go out to the island in the bay and do those opening shots. You won't have to speak, you won't even have to act very hard. It'll just be you and me and the minimum number of crew over there. No spectators. And it'll give you a chance to find your feet a little.'

'Thank you,' she said, gathering her ragged dignity around her, 'but you don't have to. If you'd rather stick to the original schedule, I'm sure I'll be fine now.' She did not know why she was thanking him, since his tone of voice made it plain that the whole exercise was sorely trying his patience. But there must have been something in her voice that tapped a small spring of human warmth in him for as he left he paused to stroke her shoulder. She felt his fingers, warm and firm, but to him the caress was nothing. He took his hand away immediately.

'I'm sure you will, Mandy. I'm sure you will. But I've decided to do it this way, and I've no intention of changing my mind twice. Now, you get a good night's sleep—I've asked them to send some supper to your room—and we'll be off at dawn tomorrow.'

It was surprising just how cold a tropical dawn could be. Bella sat in the boat and shivered, cupping her hands round a paper cup of coffee. She had her jacket wrapped round her, but Luke, sitting opposite, wore only battered navy shorts and a white T-shirt and did not seem to feel the cold. She saw the powerful muscles of his shoulders and the way the hair curled waywardly into his bronzed neck. He was conferring with Caroline over a file of papers and his head was bent close to hers. Bella watched, her eyes narrowing at the sight of their obvious intimacy, and at that moment Caroline looked up and saw her watching them. Their glances locked in hostility. Caroline was like a prize watch-dog, she thought, guarding her master, and she looked pointedly away again.

She hated being in this boat. She hated being seen as a brainless and incompetent actress. More than anything, she hated feeling this constant pull of physical attraction towards Luke Retford, when he was quite clearly a thoroughly calculating and ruthless man whom the more she knew, the more and more she disliked.

But she had to remember that it wouldn't be for long. In less than a week she would be Bella again, back at home in London, back at her desk at the institute, and this interlude would be nothing more than a lurid tropical dream.

Luke pulled her aside once they landed on the island. 'Let's walk for a bit. I want to go over what we've got to get through today.'

The sun was getting hotter by the minute. Bella

kicked off her espadrilles and shrugged away her jacket. Now she was dressed like him, in shorts and a T-shirt. He looked at her, his dark eyes with their strange inner light going over the curves of her bare shoulders.

For a moment her heart beat faster, but all he said was, 'Have you got sun block on?'

'Yes. Inches of it!' She gritted her teeth.

'Good. Now, what about your hat? Sally!'

A girl from the wardrobe department looked up from where she was checking over her boxes.

'Hat!'

She brought a large-brimmed straw sun-hat over and Luke plonked it unceremoniously on Bella's head. He grinned. 'The Quangle-Wangle!'

'You know that book?' She was startled out of her bad temper.

'I read it to my nephews. You know it?' He aped her surprise.

'I read it to my god-daughter.'

'Who's your god-daughter?' He set off, away down the beach, and she fell into step beside him. Her head came just past his shoulder.

'She's called Molly. She's three. The daughter of a colleague.'

'Another actress? Who's that?'

'No, not an actress——' She stopped short. Molly was the daughter of a senior lecturer in the institute. 'She used to be,' she said quickly, 'but she's a mum now.' Her heart was bumping, but Luke seemed not to notice.

'My nephews are three and six. Little hooligans,' he said. 'My brother believes it's good for them to run wild. They live on the Yorkshire moors and, as far as I can see, they don't wear shoes from July to

September.'

She laughed. 'I wish Molly could do that. She lives in one of those awful suburbs where children are dressed up to go to birthday parties every other day, and have to be chauffeured everywhere by car. It's no life for a child.'

They were walking steadily, and the rhythm of their steps and their conversation relaxed her. She knew enough of Luke now to know that that was exactly his intention, that he did nothing by accident, but she found she did not mind the manipulation. The sun was making the sea glow turquoise and heating the sand beneath their feet, and once they turned the corner they were alone on a perfect beach.

'Now then,' Luke said finally, and when he turned to face her she could see every trace of relaxed affability was gone, and his face was hard and his voice incisive, 'about today. Remember what this scene's all about. This is where Grayson first sees you. He's tired, stressed, middle-aged—and he hates holidays at the best of times! He's gone for a walk, and somewhere down the beach he comes across you.'

He talked for a long time, emphasising his words with his hands, drawing a vivid word picture of how he wanted her to walk and move. She was mesmerised by his voice, the powerful grace of his gestures, and swallowed as her eyes held his.

'So,' he said finally, and he put out a hand to hold her shoulder, his fingers spreading confidently over her smooth flesh, 'remember, you're keyed up, restless, excited—wanting something, but you don't know what it is. Do you know what I mean?'

She nodded. Oh, she knew what he meant! His fingers were moving lightly on her skin as he talked, in the instinctive sensuous touch of a man well-used to caressing women.

'I want you coming out of the water slowly, completely unaware you're being watched. You can push back your hair, do whatever you would do. I'm going to take some really tight close-ups, the water on your skin, your eyes, your lips, the sort of details that Grayson notices. Then you reach your towel, blot your face dry, look around, still taking in the fact that you're here at all, and throw yourself down on your beach mat.'

He pulled her a little closer, his eyes scrutinising her like camera close-ups. 'Do you understand?' His voice dropped. 'I want you very young, very beautiful, very free in your body.'

Bella felt colour rise in her cheeks. She nodded again. He tipped her chin so he could look into her face under the brim of her hat.

'Good. But I want you timid as well, and uncertain. A bit like a deer that would canter off at the slightest noise. Men like that in a woman.' He paused, his eyes roaming her purple gaze. 'Grayson senses that, which is probably why he doesn't go near you that first day. But there's something else, Mandy, underneath all that. Just think . . .' He took his hand from her chin and reclaimed her shoulder, stroking her skin. 'There you are. You're eighteen. You're lying there, on this tropical beach, in your new, sexy bikini, with the sun caressing your skin and the waves lapping at your feet. What's going on in your mind?'

She said, instantly, 'Television advertisements. You think of the girl in the chocolate bar ad. You feel like that.'

'Exactly. And what happens in that ad?'

'Um—a man comes along on a surfboard and——'

'Exactly. A man comes along. There you are,

sunbathing on this perfect beach, and it doesn't take you long to start thinking that the only thing missing from the picture is a man. And your thoughts turn to romance, and whether a man will turn up, and how nice a holiday affair would be. And that sort of thought makes you fidgety and unsatisfied.' His lips crooked ironically, as if he knew what she was feeling inside, and she had to struggle not to look away from him, thinking how apt a description that was of exactly her current state of mind, here with Luke.

His eyes scoured hers, while his fingers still moved on her skin. 'Mandy, I don't know you well enough to know how familiar you are with the feeling of straightforward physical frustration, but in this scene I want you to project a kind of restlessness, an energy that is looking for somewhere to go. I want the feeling of a girl who hardly knows her own sensuality, but who is experiencing an awakening feeling—a feeling that, with the backdrop in place, she'd like a piece of the downstage action.'

Bella swallowed, her eyes held to his, and nodded. She knew what he meant—all too well she knew what he meant! His deep, liquid voice and his compelling eyes did all that to her, and more. Not to mention the light caress of her bare shoulder, and the whole magnetic power and purpose of his presence. He looked at her more deeply, and suddenly she felt she had to lick her lips or she would no longer be able to breathe, and, when he saw the pink tip of her tongue flick nervously out, the lines that fanned from the corners of his eyes creased into a smile of confirmed triumph.

They walked back in silence and she vowed to herself to do her utmost to please Luke in this scene. She wanted to regain his respect—and, she had to admit it, arouse his desire as much as he aroused hers.

Not that it was easy. The swimming scene had to be done half a dozen times, and each time that she walked back into the sea sharp fragments of coral cut her feet. But it was surprisingly easy to walk up out of the water as Luke had instructed. The water streamed off her body and the sun kissed her skin in a way that made it impossible not to feel sensual and free, and she found that, if she thought of Luke, and how his eyes were closely following her every movement, then her languid looks and gestures came easily. After a time she even began to enjoy acting out the sensuality she had so long suppressed in her own life.

'Good girl.' The 'girl' stung her pride, but Luke's look was warmly appreciative. He came over to where Sally was renewing her essential sun block, and watched as the wardrobe girl's professional fingers lifted Bella's hair and rubbed the cream across the vulnerable nape of her neck. 'That was a good morning's work. Come and have some lunch with me when you're finished.'

'My,' said Sally, raising her eyebrows. 'You're getting the treatment. He usually takes himself off alone at meal times—to renew the creative drive!' She laughed.

'Have you worked with him before, then?'

'Oh, yes. I've been on all his pictures. He's the best—but not the easiest. He won't stand for anything less than perfection.'

'I'm finding out—look at my feet.' Bella lifted her torn soles and Sally exclaimed, 'You poor thing! Here, I've got some antiseptic cream somewhere. Why on earth didn't you say something?'

'I didn't like to complain.'

'It's not that! It's—what if they need a shot that

shows the bottom of your feet? You're lying down later, aren't you? The make-up department could try and do something to cover up the marks, if they had to, but it wouldn't be ideal.'

Bella looked at her dumbly. 'I didn't think of that.'

Sally gave her an odd look. 'I must say, for an actress you're surprisingly unvain. It makes quite a change. Maybe that's what's caught our Luke's roving eye.'

'You mean he doesn't like actresses?'

Sally laughed. 'Oh, it's not that he doesn't like them. He likes them well enough in all the usual ways, if you know what I mean. But he doesn't exactly rate them very highly as intellectual companions. He quite definitely prefers to view them from above.' She clapped her hand to her mouth. 'Oh, that sounds awful! I didn't mean it quite like that——'

'I know what you meant,' Bella said quickly, and turned away so that Sally would not see her fierce blush at the unfortunate *double entendre*. It wasn't that she was embarrassed, just that that particular image, in relation to Luke, was suddenly all too vivid for comfort.

She took a deep breath. This was ridiculous. Her attraction to him was becoming as unreal as everything else about this bizarre week. What she had to remember was what Luke was really like, why she was here, and how quickly it would all be over and her normal life resumed once more.

'I hardly think it's roving, anyway—Luke's eye. He probably wants to go over this afternoon's work.'

Sally said, 'Mmm. But you didn't see how he was looking at you just then.'

Bella walked slowly over to where Luke sprawled back on his elbows on a rug. He regarded her very

frankly, his eyes lingering over her breasts and hips in
the tight, wet bikini.

'Hat,' he commanded, as she got nearer, and she had
to turn and fetch it, knowing his eyes followed her rear
view as closely as they had observed her front one.

She stood in front of him.

'You wanted to talk to me?'

'Yes. About this afternoon.' He squinted up at her.
He had stripped off his T-shirt and now wore only
shorts. His chest was broad and strong, patterned with
dark hair which thickened into an arrow at his hips,
and his skin, next to her pale flesh, looked deeply
bronzed. 'Go and grab some salad and chicken and
come back.'

When she returned he poured her a glass of wine.
She regarded it doubtfully.

'Should I?'

'You've got no lines to fluff and it'll help to put you
in the mood.' He lifted a patently suggestive eyebrow.

She looked away. He was playing with her, she was
sure, No, not playing with her, working on her,
bolstering her faltering confidence with a charm that
he turned on and off as easily as a tap, and teasing out
her feelings by playing on the attraction he now knew
she had for him. She didn't like it, but it certainly was
effective. Her stomach clenched at his look.

'Tell me a bit more about how you see Grayson,'
she said, for something to say. 'I mean, is he just
looking for a fling, or what?' She slanted a look back
at him, her eyes a deep violet in their rims of dark
lashes.

'Grayson . . .' he began confidently, then he
suddenly faltered and stopped, as if his words were
arrested by the direct impact of her flawless beauty.
He looked at her for some seconds, and somehow she

knew he was not playing on her reaction to him any more, but was genuinely lost for words. 'Grayson,' he repeated slowly, 'isn't looking for anything, he just stumbles across it. But once it's there, he can't let it go. He just has to have it.' His eyes did not leave hers, and suddenly there was a peculiar tension rising in the air between them, as real as the pine smell of the delicate filao trees that fringed the sand behind them. The sun beat on their heads, and from somewhere down the beach came the thuds and cries of the crew playing football, but it was all distant and remote.

It was extraordinary, but in that moment all that existed was the look that passed between them, his eyes dark and lit by his thoughts, hers deep pools of purple, both gazes complex, private and unfathomable.

CHAPTER FOUR

THE day was not going well, unlike the day on the island, which had gone without a single hitch. In fact, when Bella had seen the rushes—the clips of the filming—in the viewing-room set up at the hotel, she had scarcely been able to believe her eyes.

Luke had filmed her to look, quite simply, stunning. She had had no idea she could look so sensual and beautiful, but when she had seen how she walked languidly from the water, how she lay on the beach, restlessly picking up and dropping her book, and running the sand through her hands, she had been amazed. The girl on the screen had tumbling, sun-streaked hair and perfect lips, and when she looked into the camera with her dark, purple gaze there was a sexual charge in her lingering stare that made the other viewers in the room catch their breath with the power of it.

When the lights had gone up again there had been friendly cheers and wolf whistles, and she had turned with a smile towards Luke. But he had already been leaving the room, without even a backward glance.

Guy de Vere had come over then and, seeing her look, had tried to reassure her. 'Don't worry. If Luke's got nothing to say, it must be because he's got what he wants—perfection!' He had squeezed her shoulder. 'You're a stunner, Mandy. It's going to be a great movie.'

But there was nothing great about today, Bella thought miserably. They were at the poolside, and filming was going badly. First there had been endless technical hitches, which had shaken her fragile new confidence. Then Luke, abstracted by numerous problems, had simply looked her up and down with his assessing grey gaze when she'd walked on to the set and nodded as if approving of a prize sheep.

His attitude dismayed her. Yesterday she had felt sure that something had happened between them, some deep, unspoken pull of attraction that had made her glow and flower for him under the cameras like a fragile tropical bloom opening in the sun. Now, though, she began to wonder if it had all been some figment of her fevered imagination.

They had run through the scene one time, but, although she had managed to speak her lines, she knew it had gone badly. Guy de Vere had been confident and professional, but her responses to him had been tight and wooden. When he had settled himself at her table and started to exert his charm on her she had been unable to respond, and Luke had called a halt.

Now he clapped his hands. 'OK. Take a break, everybody.' He sighed. 'Mandy. Over here.' Bella followed his beckoning arm meekly and they began to walk away from the set, over the sand towards the sea.

'What's the matter?' His tone was blunt. 'You were fabulous yesterday. Today you're exuding as much sex appeal as a plank of wood.'

She shook her head, wanting to cry. How could she tell him the truth—that she was no actress, and that Guy de Vere's Hollywood charms made her *feel* like a plank of wood? That there was no electricity when she looked at him, no charge in their glances?

She glanced at Luke and their glances snagged, and suddenly it was all there again for her, all the electricity and the charge she could possibly handle.

He stopped and stared down at her, looking at her

properly for the first time that day, and she saw his thoughts turning keenly, his eyes darkening. They were blue this morning, she saw shakily, not grey, but blue like the sea against the tan of his face, and his lips were firm and even. He took a long moment before he spoke. His expression was tense and there was a tone in his voice that made her guess he was struggling to master both anger and impatience.

'Look,' he said slowly, 'forget the people, forget Guy if it makes it easier. Remember what we talked about yesterday? The girl in the chocolate advertisement? Well, that's you. You're young, you're alone, you're restless, you're wanting something . . .' His voice grew less harsh and he casually reached out and caught her elbow, trailing his fingers down the soft inside of her arm to her wrist as he talked. It was an exquisite touch, experienced and sensual, and it sent her blood pulsing under his light fingers until her lips parted involuntarily at the feeling he was rousing in her. He grinned a little when he saw the changes in her look. 'There,' he said, and his voice was lower, rougher, 'You see—you can do it any time you want to, you just have to let your thoughts roam free. Unhitch them and set them loose, and they'll do all your work for you.'

He was smiling, she could see the whiteness of his teeth as he talked, and mocking her gently as if he could see where her thoughts were roaming. She flushed. She was thinking about kisses, the drag of teeth on soft flesh, and she was sure he must know.

'Now think about it, the scene you've got to do this morning,' he went on, in the same roughened voice. 'Your skin has been heated up by the sun, your inhibitions have been diluted by a couple of pina coladas, the sea is blue, the sand is white, you've got no ties. You know you're beautiful . . .' His fingers were still moving on her skin and he stepped closer, as if he would pull her round into his arms. She felt breathless at his nearness, the overwhelming power of him, and she could feel her lips softening and her eyes growing larger as he seduced her with his voice and his touch. 'Then along comes this older man whom you're a little bit wary of, but who is nevertheless attractive and sophisticated and quite different from the boys you've known, and you quickly fall under his spell.' Now his hand moved up her arm, to grasp her shoulder as his eyes held hers. Her blood was beating as he said, low and intimately, 'You're as ripe as a little plum waiting to be picked, and you're only too glad to let Grayson be the harvester.'

She was in a spell, entranced by his words, his voice, aching inside at the way he roused her longings, when suddenly there was a shout of laughter and, tearing her eyes from his, she saw over his shoulder a couple of the crew joking and pointing towards their two linked figures. She tore herself from him, crying bitterly, 'You make me sound like an object, not a person!'

He was unperturbed. 'Not in the slightest—after all, remember what happens in the end. You so enslave Grayson that it's he who comes running after you——' his eyes forced hers back to his '—but all that comes later, much later. Now is now.' He searched her face and a taunting smile crept slowly back into his eyes, daring her to share his conspiracy. 'It's all there, isn't it, Mandy? You know and I know. It's all there inside you. It just has to be set free.' He paused, his eyes still roaming her face. 'What you must do is to forget all about Guy, put someone else there in his place—someone you could really fancy.' A lazy grin crooked his lips. 'That's the answer for you, Mandy.'

Think about someone you could really fancy, and the rest will be a piece of cake.'

He was right, of course. Bella reflected later that he knew his job all too well. When she thought of him, when she imagined it was Luke, not Guy, who was chatting her up at the poolside, then her body and face seemed to act of their own accord. After just two more takes the scene was in the can and Guy was showing a whole new interest in his youthful co-star.

'Mandy, honey, come and have lunch?' he drawled.

'No, thank you, Guy. I need a rest.'

'You can rest over a cold drink. Look all the sensible people are heading for the bar.'

Bella followed his look and saw Luke and Caroline walking up the steps. Caroline, looking slim and cool in a lemon minidress and rakish white baseball cap, had her arm linked in Luke's and was talking earnestly, while Luke bent his head down to listen.

She watched them disappear. 'Is it like that, Guy?' She tried to nod casually at the departing couple. 'I thought she was just his assistant.'

He shrugged. 'I guess so. They've been around together a long time.'

'Oh.'

He laughed. 'What else is there to do—stuck out on film sets for weeks at a time?'

'I see.'

Something in her tight tone made him pause.

'Ah, now, come on, honey. Don't you go wasting your time getting interested in Luke Retford. The man's a workaholic for one thing.'

'I wasn't.' She laughed lightly. 'I was just surprised. They seem so different.'

He pulled a face, his eyes hardening. 'She's not my type, that's for sure. Too tight——' he checked himself

'— well, I won't say the word in front of a lady.'

She laughed, genuinely this time. 'I can guess what you mean, and I think I agree.'

'How about that drink?'

'No, really, Guy. I'm off for a siesta.'

She thought about Guy as she lay naked under a sheet in her darkened room, a fan stirring the thick air above her head. Most women in the world would love to be invited to lunch by this great Hollywood sex symbol, she thought, yet all she could think of was how much he perspired and how his breath was laden with the scent of his cigars.

While Luke, in contrast, only had to shoot her one glance from under his dark brows to send the blood thudding along her veins. She shut her eyes and felt again his fingers on her arm, caressing her soft skin.

She moved her legs restlessly, cursing her thoughts. She wanted to put him out of her mind, but she could not. Everything seemed to conspire against her, turning her thoughts to sensual delights. The soft cotton against her bare skin, the stir of drugged heat, the whisper of the palm fronds outside the window, all made her feel sultry and unsatisfied. The island was so exotic, so lovely, it seemed to demand passion and romance, and even while she hated his arrogance, of his arms the casual way he manipulated her feelings, she could not deny that her body had a mind of its own and longed to know the embrace of his arms and the press of his lips.

She turned on her stomach and thrust her hands into her hair, shocked at the vivid destination her imaginings led her to. Ever since her affair with Nick had broken up, all those years ago, she had lived quietly and celibately, putting all her energy into building her career.

She had never been tempted to stray from her chosen path, and the memory of the lonely months after Nick had told her that their engagement was off, that he didn't want to marry her, or anyone, for many years to come, still had the power to hurt.

At least, they had had.

Now she tested out her most painful recollections gingerly, like someone standing for the first time on a healed broken leg, and found to her amazement that they no longer hurt!

The astonishment made her sit up with a start. She tried again, remembering the worst time of all, when Nick, who had been furious at her unwillingness to accept his decision, had hurled endless accusations at her —that she was as clinging as a Russian vine, that it was not him she wanted, just anyone to settle down with, that she was old and staid before she was young—and the same was true. The cure was complete. She could examine them quite objectively now, understanding clearly for the first time that, while some of the things he had said were true, others had been just part of his defensive need to attack her.

About Nick himself, she also felt quite neutral now, she discovered. They had met as students, and had had a happy, steady relationship for two long years. She had loved him then, in a low-key way, and had always assumed she still did. But now she had to frown hard to bring his blond good looks to mind, and she realised with a sudden joyous rush of release that if she met him again he would hold little interest for her any more.

For it was true what he had said—she *had* been old before her time and more than a little staid, while he had been a safe harbour for a pretty but studious nineteen-year-old, alone for the first time in London.

As a twin she had always known the comfort of Mandy at her side, but Mandy had gone off to act in York, leaving her alone and uncertain how to handle the numerous male advances that came her way. Nick had simply walked in and taken over, and she had been more than happy to let him.

But she did not want safety now: she wanted something else. She wanted excitement, passion, danger. She wanted the despicable Luke.

'Oh!' She groaned into her pillow at the tangle of her thoughts. Because, although Luke was quite obviously willing to beam his considerable charms in her direction when it suited him, his interest in her never lasted beyond those short moments. And even if it did—what then? Would she really want him, anyway, a man as ruthless as that? And, even if she did, where would it all lead? After all, she could hardly have a torrid entanglement with him here in Mauritius, and then fly off and leave Mandy to take up where she had left off.

To cool her fevered imagination she forced herself to think of Caroline, as cold and frosty as an icicle. But there must be times when even Caroline let herself go, she thought—who knew, maybe even at this very moment? Did she and Luke retire together during the heat of the day? And, if so, did he tumble those glossy tresses into disarray and set a flush on that porcelain skin? Presumably he must, because she could not imagine that a man as sensual as he clearly was would settle for anything less than the ultimate fire and passion.

'Oh,' she groaned again, tugging at her hair to bring herself to her senses. It was no good. She had to put thoughts of Luke to one side, or she would go crazy with this adolescent crush. After all, it was only stand-in Mandy who wanted him. The cool and scientific mind of Bella Latham wanted nothing whatever to do with the man!

To calm herself, and to anchor herself back in reality, she got up and fetched a draft of the lecture that she was due to give at the major medical conference in Bristol next month, and made herself start to read it carefully. but a knock interrupted her thoughts. Her heart hammered.

'Yes?'

'Mandy?'

Bella's heart hammered twice as hard.

'Yes.'

'You decent?'

'I——er——'

The door was already opening. 'Well, pull the sheet up.'

Luke came in, straight over to the bed. She flushed guiltily, and struggled to anchor the sheet under her arms while setting her papers down quickly on the far side of the bed.

He regarded her actions curiously, but said nothing.

'Could you pass my T-shirt, please?' she got out primly.

He handed her the white garment and turned his back while she slipped it on.

'Thank you.'

'You weren't asleep, then?'

'No.'

'And you weren't having a drink with Guy, either?' His eyes were dark, unfathomable.

'How did you know he'd asked me?'

'He came and joined us at the bar. Announced he'd been turned down by you.' Casually he sat down on her bed. She could feel his weight close to her bare legs beneath the thin sheet. 'I can't say I blame you. No one has just one drink with Guy. It always turns into a marathon drinking session.'

'I'm surprised you allow it.'

'Oh, Guy can carry his drink—most of the time, anyway. And he'd probably walk out if I put him on the wagon.' His eyes went over hers. 'What about you? Do you drink much?'

'No, not much. Why?'

He shrugged. 'Just curious. I don't know much about you, Mandy, and I feel I need to. If we're going to work together, I have to know what makes you tick.'

He put out a casual hand and pushed back a lock of Bella's hair. His fingers were cool and light on her forehead.

'Is that the reason for your visit? To see what makes me tick?' Her voice was tight with strain at his nearness.

'If you like. I also wanted to run over this afternoon's scene with you.'

'Well, you're wasting your time. I've got no deep, dark secrets!' Her voice was too high for comfort. She struggled to bring it down. 'I'm just an ordinary actress——'

His eyes flicked quickly round her room, over the piles of files and books, the work she had brought with her from the institute. Then they rested on her again.

'Everyone has secrets, and no one's ordinary—least of all you.'

'What do you mean?'

'Don't be so defensive. You're as jumpy as a cat.' He looked at her in a way that made her tremble secretly, beneath the sheet. 'What I mean is, you're one of the sexiest women I've ever worked with.

There's a special quality about you, Mandy, something shy and elusive——it's almost as if you're afraid of your own sensuality, your own emotions. You keep them all locked up tight and hidden away. But then, when they spill out—phew! It almost scorches the screen.'

Bella lowered her eyes, unable to meet his look any longer.

'Mandy——' his hand was on her arm '——I'm not giving you a line. It's the truth, believe me. I've filmed hundreds of women who think that they're sexy just because they've got pouting lips and a generous cleavage, but it's nothing to do with any of that. It's something else, something that comes from the inside, from what that person is——'

'I didn't know you were such an expert!'

'On women?' He smiled. 'It's one area where I do claim some expertise. In the professional sense, of course.'

'Oh, of course. In the professional sense.'

She raised her eyes and he smiled at her, and she found herself smiling back, and suddenly it was all there again, a feeling between them as thick as the hot air turned by the lazy fan above her bed. His smile faded, but his eyes held hers and she saw his lips part a little, as if he were taking breath. And she held herself as still as a statue, wondering if he could possibly be about to bend down and kiss her.

But as her heart beat away the silent seconds there was another sharp rap on the door. 'Make-up! Ten minutes!'

'Oh!'

He let go of her arm and leaned back. 'Ten minutes,' he repeated slowly. 'Then we'd better get down to some work on this afternoon's scene.'

Later, much later, she walked alone in the heavy

tropical twilight that was fading rapidly to velvet night. They had worked all afternoon on the same scene, until she had finally felt things starting to come together, with her body moving languorously of its own accord and her voice husky with yearning. Adrenalin had started to pump through her veins as she'd recognised the power she had to make the script on the page come alive, and Guy had seemed to spark towards her with fresh warmth. It was heady to know she could do it, and Luke's warm, 'Good, Mandy, good' had been balm to her ears.

She supposed this was why Mandy put up with it all, the poverty and uncertainty of her chosen career. Because, when it started to work, it was like a rush of the headiest drug imaginable.

Now she was walking along the long white beach that seemed to stretch from the hotel to the end of the world. Once she was round the corner the lights that twinkled among the palm trees were hidden and she was alone in her tropical paradise.

She had sped away at the end of the filming, anxious not to be caught by any of the crew and swept off to the bar. People were already beginning to think her distant and stuck-up, she knew, but that was a million times better than having her awful ignorance of their world revealed. And, although Mandy had issued her with copious briefing notes before she'd caught the plane out here, they had both agreed that the safest thing of all would be for her to have as few social contacts as possible.

She stopped and looked around, at the last slivers of sunset on the tropical waters and the slender trunks of the palms, like dark cut-outs against the eggshell sky. Dusk fell heavily in the tropics and the night seemed to fold about her.

The little waves broke gently at her feet as she walked at the water's edge. The sea was like a warm bath on her bare feet, caressing her skin in its silky embrace, and suddenly she wanted to be part of it, embraced by the water in the tropical twilight.

The beach out here was deserted. She could see for miles, and there was no one about. It was a matter of seconds to untwist the sarong she had worn for this afternoon's scene and plunge naked into the water, glorying in the way the sea soothed her heated limbs.

She swam a long way out, almost to where the sea broke over the coral reef, then back towards the shore, turning to float on her back and look at the stars. The water played over her naked limbs, whispering cool and intimate, and after a time it seemed to flow through her head, calming her thoughts and freeing them to float where they would.

For years now she had driven herself non-stop, anxious to do well in her chosen field. Mandy teased her about the dullness of dry statistics, but to Bella researching the patterns of different types of illnesses had a fascination all its own. She knew she was good at her work, and she wanted to make the fullest contribution she could.

She had willingly spent her holidays working, or attending conferences and seminars, anxious to make the most of every opportunity. And in the years since her affair with Nick there had been no men in her life to distract her, only plenty of offers which she had rejected automatically.

Nick. She tried to bring him to mind, but instead she found herself remembering the touch of Luke's fingers on her arm. All the energy and sensuality that was in him had communicated itself to her in that light touch, and in the rough, caressing rasp of his voice. No doubt that had been his exact intention. But it had worked. 'Think of someone you could really fancy,' he had instructed her, this morning, and he had known, full well, that it was him.

Was that why he had come to her room this afternoon? To rouse her senses some more? She did not know, but she knew how much she had longed for him to kiss her, and it frightened her, this power he had over her body. She was drawn to him like a magnet. No one had ever conjured inside her such desperate desire before. The loving between her and Nick had been good enough, but never, ever like this brute, primitive longing that Luke aroused.

She stirred her hands in the dark sea, while above her the stars trembled and pulsed. They were beautiful, a vast vault of glittering light that arched all around her, so different from the pale pinpoints that passed for stars in the smoggy night sky of London that they could have been different objects altogether. Just as Luke's driving sexuality was a different order of energy from the friendly passion of Nick, which was the only kind she had ever known.

CHAPTER FIVE

EVENTUALLY Bella swam back towards the shore. Darkness had fallen and the moon was a huge globe in the sky. When she stood up in the shallows, with the water streaming from her full breasts and slender hips, the silver light turned her into an ethereal figure, remote and beautiful.

'Stunning. Simply stunning.'

It was only a murmur, but it carried as clear as a bell across the silent water. Her head shot round. A part of the darkness had detached itself from the shadows of the black coconut palms and was walking slowly down the sand towards her. It was Luke.

For a moment panic seized her. There was nowhere to run, nowhere to hide. And Luke was sauntering quite openly towards her. The effrontery! she thought.

Then, from nowhere, the very devil seemed to seize her. After all, she had done nothing wrong. She had nothing to hide. And hadn't Luke himself told her she was beautiful?

Slowly she reached up with both hands and smoothed the hair back from her forehead. The movement lifted her breasts, and emphasised the perfect curve of her waist and hips. She shook her hair free and began to wade languidly towards the shore.

As she got nearer, she lifted her head and met Luke's eyes with a bold and taunting gaze quite new to her. A wriggle of heady excitement went through her at the burning way he gazed back at her, and their looks held steadily until she reached the sand.

Luke looked at her, his gaze going frankly over her

breasts and hips.

'I took a nude scene out of the movie,' he murmured. 'Maybe I should put it back. It seems almost criminal to deprive people of such beauty.' His eyes were black pits, his voice roughened.

'I didn't sign to do nude scenes!'

Now that she was close to him, her courage began to ebb, and her voice was sharp with nerves. She turned away and caught up her sarong swiftly from the sand.

'No.' His hand grasped her wrist. 'Don't put that on. The colours may run, and we need it again tomorrow. Where's your towel?'

'I don't have one. I only came for a walk. But the sea looked so inviting I went in on impulse.'

Her heart was beating crazily from the grasp of his fingers on her arm. They were so close she could smell the freshness of his skin, the curling dampness of his hair. He wore only jeans and a white shirt, his feet were bare in the sand, and she guessed he must have showered and changed before coming for a walk along the beach.

'Then have this.'

He let her go and unbuttoned his shirt. His chest was tanned and strong, patterned with curling dark hair. She swallowed. He swung it behind her and helped her into the sleeves, tugging the collar into place at her throat. She swallowed again. Her throat felt tight and dry.

'Why will we need it again? The sarong? We've finished that scene,' she croaked.

'Oh, no, we haven't.'

'What?' she was aghast. 'But you said it was good!'

'Good isn't good enough.'

'It was working, I know it was. I felt it,' she protested.

His eyes bored down on her. 'Yes, but I need you to feel it even more.'

Something in his tone, an almost menacing innuendo, made her body beat beneath his look. His eyes scoured hers before he spoke.

'Mandy, you're a sensual woman, I know it. Yet when you get in front of the cameras you always seem to hold something back.'

'You don't know the first thing about me!'

'I know you're a creature of impulse, of passion. Look at you now!' He nodded down at Bella's nakedness, glimmering in the moonlight. 'The night seduced you, the water beckoned you, and without a second thought you threw off all your clothes and jumped in.'

'I thought I was alone. I would never have done it if I had known there was anyone about.'

'No?' He lifted a sceptical eyebrow. 'I didn't notice you ducking down beneath the water with modest shyness when I appeared. Rather the opposite, I would have said——'

'I don't know what you're talking about!'

'Don't you?' He mocked her with his eyes. 'If I were very unkind, I would have said you were flaunting yourself at me.'

'Don't flatter yourself! All I was doing was walking back to the beach. And as for modesty—it was a bit late for that, wasn't it, with you staring at me so openly? You could have had the decency to just keep walking.'

He shook his head, smiling a little grimly at her. 'No. That wasn't an option, not after I'd seen you. You don't see Aphrodite rising from the waves and simply walk on by without another glance!'

'Aphrodite!' she scorned.

'You didn't see yourself, Mandy. You didn't see how unutterably lovely you looked. And as for the flaunting—if it was designed to be arousing, then it had exactly the effect you intended.' He pulled her closer, his hands still holding the two sides of her shirt collar, and she quivered, helpless beneath his look, now knowing what he intended.

For a long moment he looked down into Bella's violet gaze, her lashes clumped with water, and she heard him take a sharp breath. 'You are so beautiful, so perfect——'

'Don't,' she got out.

'When I saw you there, knee-deep in water, so free and unselfconscious, I wanted to drag you up on to the sand and make love to you as fiercely as I know how! I'll make no bones about it! Why should I?' Her imagination leapt wildly, along with the blood in her veins, at his words. 'If you had but known it,' he said wickedly, 'there was no need at all for that elaborate pantomime.'

'Oh, how dare you?'

She tried to pull free, but his hands still held the shirt collar.

'Not that I'm complaining,' he added, unmoved by her anger. 'I enjoyed the show.'

'I wouldn't put on a show for you if you were the last man on earth!'

'No?' His eyes dismissed her lie, and as he held her gaze he slowly began to trail his hands down the open front of her shirt. She shivered deeply as the backs of his fingers grazed the sensitive curves of her breasts. It was a butterfly touch, so experienced and subtle that she could not be sure she had really felt it. But her body knew differently and filled and tightened towards him.

'Oh!' She could not stop herself from gasping at the

sensation.

'Call it arrogance,' he drawled provocatively, 'but I somehow find it hard to believe I leave you entirely unmoved.' And his hands stole round her naked waist to pull her to him.

His embrace was sure and firm, his fingers spreading possessively across the smooth skin of her back.

'Don't——' she got out again, turning her head aside, although her mind was spinning at his nearness and her body yearned to press closer to his.

For a moment he released the pressure, leaving her free to step away from him. 'Why? Is there someone else? Someone back in London?'

Somehow she did not step back, and his hands still spread across her back.

'It's not that. It's——'

'Nothing worth worrying about,' he murmured firmly, and pulled her back into his arms. 'Look around, Mandy, there's no one else in the whole universe. Just you and me and the sea and sand, the moon and stars. And sometimes in life you just have to push common sense aside and seize the moment before the world turns on its way again and it's gone before you've grasped it——' Even as he spoke, he bent his head and found her mouth, opening it surely with his lips.

'Oh!'

Immediately she was lost in a sea of sensation, the feeling of his kiss, the touch of his embrace. She knew she should pull away, but instead she yielded to him, her breasts knowing the rasp of hair on his naked chest, her mind reeling from the raw desire he inflamed in her.

She closed her eyes, giving herself up to the

feelings, letting him deepen his embrace. He pulled her more tightly to him, exploring the sweetness of her mouth, his hands roaming the curves of her back.

'Mandy,' he groaned against her mouth, 'I can't remember when I've wanted a woman so much.'

Mandy! She forced her eyes open. She was not Mandy, she was Bella! She was right at the centre of a tangled web of fragile deceit, and here was Luke walking right through her pitiful defences to the deceiving heart of it!

'What is it?' He pulled back. She looked at him and her heart tore with loss. She had never seen a man so handsome as Luke looked at this moment, his eyes glittering and dark, his mouth brooding with desire.

'Stop it—leave me alone.'

He stepped back, holding up his arms in a parody of surrender, his eyes hard. 'But why, Mandy? You're a woman, not a child.'

'I——'

He put up an abrasive hand. 'And don't tell me you're not interested. We've just set each other aflame!'

'I know what you're doing!'

'I would have thought that was entirely obvious—to anyone with even an elementary knowledge of human biology.' He pushed a hand through his hair, his eyes glittering. 'I would love to make love to you, I'll admit it. But I'm not in the habit of forcing women to do anything against their will—if that's what you're worrying about. You only have to say stop . . .' He shrugged eloquently.

She turned away, forcing her own, coolly logical mind to the fore.

'It's not me you're interested in. Oh, yes, you wouldn't mind making love to me because you've happened to stumble across me like this— and because it's a deserted beach and a moonlit tropical night——' Her voice choked, then gathered strength again. 'But I'm no fool. I know what you really want!'

'Oh. And what's that?' His voice was harsh, dangerous.

'You want to work on me, loosen me up, get me to behave the way you want me to in front of the cameras!' She spun round, accusing him with her eyes. 'You know Guy doesn't turn me on, so you've decided to put in a little groundwork of your own. You've been doing it for days—all those looks, those touches. It works, I'll admit it, but I'm not stupid enough to think it's real! And I'm certainly not stupid enough to allow myself to do anything foolish because of it——!'

'Is it always stupid to be foolish?' His voice cut in like a knife.

'What do you mean?' She was thrown

He stepped forward, gripping her arm, his words coming fast. 'I mean, have you always been so cold, Mandy Latham? Have you always let your head rule your heart? Put cool logic before hot passion? Look around you——' he flung out a hand at the stars that arched overhead '—you're right, it's a deserted beach and a tropical night. And we're a man and a woman— what could be more natural than turning into each other's arms? It's not a crime—whatever the reasons!'

She dragged her arm away. 'You can't deny what I've just said! For all I know you followed me down the beach on purpose——'

'Is that what you really think?'

'I wouldn't put it past you. I think you'd do anything, almost anything at all, to make a better movie!'

For a moment there was silence, then he grinned grimly. 'Maybe you understand me better than I thought,' he conceded, 'but I'll tell you something.' His grin faded into a look of such harsh sternness that she quailed beneath it. 'First of all, I came along the beach to be alone—just as you did. I didn't look for this, I'm not sure I even wanted it to happen. Secondly, I could never pretend attraction towards a woman who did not stir me, and I certainly could never begin to make love to one I did not desire.' His gaze ripped over her for a moment. 'I might be many things, but a commercial gigolo is not one of them!'

Her gaze blazed back at him, deepest violet shot througfh with angry fire.. 'And is that supposed to answer the question?'

'It isn't supposed to do anything except tell you how I feel!'

She summoned all her reserves of dignity and icy anger.

'Thank you,' she bit out. 'I'll remember to bear it in mind. And now, if you'll excuse me——' And, snatching up her sarong, she pushed past him and ran across the beach.

In the morning Bella hoped it was all a terrible dream, but the first thing she saw when she opened her eyes was Luke's white shirt hanging like a flag on the chair by her bed.

'Oh, no!' She squeezed her eyes shut. What exactly had happened last night? Vivid flashes of memory danced across her brain—pulsing stars and warm sand under her toes, and the feeling, the powerful feeling, of Luke's embrace. And then their angry, shouting words.

What madness had possessed her, to let him kiss her

like that, and then to spurn him so angrily? Because now his contempt for her acting skills would be fuelled even further by his fury at her accusations about his behaviour. And the bad situation she was already in would deteriorate still further.

There was an angry banging on the door.

'Come in.'

Caroline marched in, cool and superior in a cream linen shift. 'Still in bed, Mandy? You must have had a late night.'

'What do you want, Caroline?'

'Luke has sent me looking for his laundry. I gather he had to rescue a damsel in distress last night.'

'You gather wrong.' Bella pushed herself up in the bed and tried to smooth her hair into some sort of order. She saw Caroline take in her tousled beauty and scowl.

'You know, you're wasting your time chasing Luke,' she said waspishly. 'Oh, he'll be interested for a time—until he gets what he wants—but don't expect it to last.'

'The shirt is there, Caroline,' Bella said pointedly. 'Why don't you take it and go?'

With insolent slowness the girl sauntered round and gathered it up. Then she sauntered back, scrutinising closely the contents of the room. 'You do a lot of reading.' She nodded at the piles of books and files stacked on the dressing-table.

'Is it a crime?'

Caroline turned slowly. 'Take a piece of advice from a friend—consider Luke Retford off limits.'

'Is that a threat? My, how melodramatic!'

'It's for your own good.'

'That's what people always say when they're looking after their own interests!'

Caroline laughed nastily. 'My interests are perfectly well looked after already, thank you.'

'Oh, really?' Bella arched her eyebrows. 'Then why do you need to worry about me?'

'Oh, I'm not worried, Mandy. I've seen it all before. Beautiful little actresses getting all starry-eyed about the Great God Director. It happens every time. They come and go. I doubt if Luke can tell one from another after a time. I just hate to see women making fools of themselves—and when it comes to flinging themselves into the water naked in front of him——'

'I did no such thing!' Anger propelled Bella out of the bed. She flung on her robe and swirled around. 'Did Luke tell you that?'

Caroline arched her brows. 'It doesn't take much to work it out.'

'I'll tell you what happened last night, exactly what happened! I went for a walk and, because I thought I was alone, I went for a swim. I had no idea Luke was anywhere around, and if I'd known I would never have dreamed of going in. But he was, he saw me, and he insisted I wear his shirt because he didn't want to risk having the sarong spoilt for today's filming. That's what happened. Now why don't you take the shirt and go?' She flung the door open pointedly.

Caroline stood without moving, her arms crossed. 'You forget how well I know Luke.'

'And what's that supposed to mean?'

'You know what it means.'

Guilty colour flushed her cheeks at the sudden memory of how Luke's hands had grazed her breasts.

'If you're saying we had a night of wild passion out there on the sand, you couldn't be more wrong!'

'Oh, I'm not saying that. Luke came home like a bear with a sore head and sat up all night working. A sure sign he'd been thwarted!'

Bella's heart twisted at Caroline's words. So Luke had returned to her room last night, after their row on the beach.

'So what's your problem?'

'I never thought you were the type for a one-night stand, Mandy. But, if last night was the opening shot of your campaign, you might as well forget it. There's no point in stringing Luke along in the hope of something more. He doesn't have the time, or the inclination!'

However unfair her words, they hit home, with a pain through Bella's heart. Caroline saw it and pressed home her advantage.

'You see, Mandy, he's got me, and he's got his work. He doesn't need anything else. You might as well realise that now, and save yourself a lot of time and trouble.'

'The only person who's giving me trouble is you,' she said tightly. 'Now, if you'll excuse me . . .'

Caroline walked slowly towards the door, pausing to look scornfully over her. Bella burned under the girl's contemptuous look, and anger flared higher inside her. 'Of course, the thing you ought to ask yourself,' she flung out scornfully, 'is just why you feel the need to warn people off your boyfriend. Or isn't he quite as happy to stay at home with you as you'd like?'

And, to Bella's satisfaction, Caroline's cheeks flushed with colour as she hurried away.

Luke came straight over and took Bella's elbow as she walked on to the set. 'Hello, Mandy, recovered from your moonlight swim?'

She looked him straight in the eye. 'There was nothing to recover from.'

It wasn't true. The very sight of Luke, dressed this morning in a black T-shirt and shorts, made her feel almost sick with longing.

He grinned—those sensual lips, and white teeth . . . 'There was for me,' he confessed frankly. 'I was far too frustrated to sleep. Every time I shut my eyes I saw your beautiful figure rising from the waves again!'

She burned under his look, as his eyes devoured her face, but she held herself rigid.

'I wish we had made love last night,' he confessed, with a frank grin, 'and not just for my own state of health—it would have done wonders for your nervous tension!'

'There you go again,' she said tensely, and he raised an eyebrow, mocking both himself and her. And suddenly, somehow, they were laughing together and all the bad feelings between them, the anger and frustration, were transformed into mutual acknowledgment of the game they were both caught up in.

'Now, about this morning,' he said finally, their eyes still smiling together, 'will you give it all you've got, Mandy, please? All I now know you've got,' he added in a conspiratorial voice, and she responded readily.

'I'll try my best.'

And he'd done it again, she thought later, because this morning it all came easily, until the scene between her and Guy positively pulsed with the electric charge of sexual tension. There was silence all around as the cameras rolled, and the scene unfolded to its climax, and in her head was the clear memory of Luke's hands on her naked back and his lips exploring hers.

'Phew,' said Guy afterwards. 'I suppose it was an open secret to everyone here just how much I enjoyed that, Mandy. You'll be a star!'

'How was it?' Bella asked, walking directly over to Luke, her eyes dancing with triumph.

'How do you think?'

'It felt OK.'

'OK,' he mocked her. 'The girl just about burns up the camera lens, and she says it feels "OK".' Swiftly, unexpectedly, he bent and brushed his lips across the corner of her mouth. 'You were terrific, Mandy. Two hundred per cent "OK"—at least!'

'Luke.' Caroline materialised beside them. 'We have to go through the schedules.'

Luke dropped his arm from Bella's back and took the papers. 'OK. We'll work over lunch.' He pushed a hand through his hair and she looked at him and saw black smudges under his eyes. Had she really caused him a sleepless night? The thought teased excitement beneath her ribs. But, even as she looked at him, Caroline was urging him away.

But he stopped, turning back to her. 'We'll have a night off tonight, to celebrate. All of us. I'll get something fixed up at the hotel down the road.'

CHAPTER SIX

GUY sidled up and put his arm around Bella. 'Come and have lunch with me.'

'Oh, I thought I'd rest——' she began, but as she spoke Luke slanted a dark, questioning glance back at their two figures, and somehow she found herself trilling loudly, 'But why not? I'd love lunch, Guy.'

He took her to a shady table on the poolside terrace, well away from the other lunchers.

'Here's to a rousing performance,' he said, lifting his glass and winking wickedly at her. 'At least, it roused me.'

She blushed, knowing full well what he meant, and said hastily, 'Luke gave me a talking to last night. It would have been more than my life was worth not to pull something out of the bag.'

'Oh, Luke, Luke!' he mourned, meaningfully.

'You've done a lot of work with him, haven't you? You must know him pretty well.'

'Yup. Four movies, this is our fifth. He's the best there is. But, young Mandy——' his eyes went over her shrewdly '—he's death for women.'

'What do you mean?'

'I mean what I've told you before—there's only one real love in Luke's life, and that's his movies. Women fall for him like ninepins—all that dark intensity packed into a frame that half of Hollywood would be proud of—but it's wasted effort——'

'You mean he's not interested?'

He laughed. 'Oh, he's a perfectly normal red-blooded male, if that's what you're asking. Women come and go,

78

but woe betide any of them who hope for more than a temporary liaison. They hardly last at all. If Luke doesn't give them the big E, Caroline does it for him. She's an expert at seeing off the opposition.'

I know, Bella thought, remembering the unpleasant little scene in her room that morning, but all she said was, 'Luke seems to rely on her a lot.'

'He couldn't function without her. She's like an extra limb. I've told him he ought to do the inevitable, and make an honest woman of her!' He laughed heartily and Bella smiled stiffly.

'Most successful men have a good woman behind them,' she said, switching from the painful subject. 'Who's yours?'

He eyed her oddly. 'You must have read the Press about me and Veronica.'

Dimly she remembered that Mandy's crib sheets had included a note on his recent marriage break-up, but she had not bothered to read it in detail because she had not planned to socialise with Guy de Vere.

'Oh—yes. I'm sorry, that was tactless.'

'It's OK. My life's an open book. Always has been. There'll be no nasty secrets to rake over when I'm dead and gone.'

She smiled more warmly. He was a nice man, in some ways. He crinkled his eyes back at her. 'Tell me about yourself, Mandy. Where were you this time last week—month—year?'

'Out of work, out of work, out of work!' Bella rolled her eyes dramatically, and out of the corner of them she saw Luke walking over with Caroline. 'You can't believe how pleased I was to get this job!' she breathed fervently, and batted her eyelashes flirtatiously in Guy's direction.

His famous blue eyes sparkled at her in instant response.

'Did you think of quitting?'

'No, never.'

'That's the spirit. You need grit and staying power more than anything else in this business. But you must have done some work——'

'Mainly provincial theatres. Nothing interesting,' she said quickly, 'Tell me about you—you're such a huge star now, it's hard to believe you were ever on the bottom rung.'

As Mandy had correctly predicted, no one would bother about her reticence if offered the chance to talk about themselves, and Guy launched immediately into his life story, but a dark shadow fell across their table, cutting off his flow. She looked up into Luke's narrowed eyes and her stomach lurched.

'Guy, I'm taking away one beautiful woman and giving you another,' he said smoothly. 'I'm afraid I need Mandy to do some work—but Caroline will keep you company.'

Caroline smiled sourly at Guy, who looked briefly irritated, then masked it with his ready smile. 'My pleasure,' he drawled.

Luke lifted her and steered her swiftly away between the tables with a hand at her elbow. 'I've done a quick bit of rejigging, put in a couple of extra scenes,' he told her rapidly. 'You were so out of this world this morning that I want to give you a bigger part. I want more of what you had going this morning—as much as you can possibly give.'

He led her towards the thatched bungalow that was being used as the indoor set of Grayson's hotel room.

'Now listen hard, because we've only got a short time. Union rules. The crew won't carry on past four o'clock today without new agreements.'

He turned her to him, and emphasised his words

with chopping motions of his hands.

'Now listen, Dee's come back here, with Grayson, to his hotel room. It's hot, the blinds are down. He's brought you in here, maybe kissed you once or twice—the audience will have to assume all that—and now he's left you alone for a minute while he goes to the bathroom.'

He grinned at her wickedly. 'Let's assume he downed a beer or two for Dutch courage before setting off to find you on the beach, and now his middle-aged bladder is letting him down.'

She smiled back, but her grin faded as he demanded, 'How do you think you'd be feeling, at such a moment?'

She thought, searching his eyes with her own wide lavender gaze. She saw a movement in his throat as he swallowed under her look. 'A bit nervous?'

'Maybe. What else?'

She thought. What if it were she and someone she had really fallen for? She and Luke? How would she feel then? She flushed a little. 'Excited, keyed up, frightened that it was all going to fade. Impatient for him to come back——'

He held her shoulders, his touch warm on her bare arms, his eyes still searching hers. 'Good. Go on.'

Her blood stirred and began to throb in her veins as she held his eyes. They were standing close together in the hot, languorous room, with the bed like an invitation beside them, and suddenly the air seemed to be charged with far more than just the imaginary atmosphere that Luke was summoning up.

'You *do* know the feeling?' Luke quizzed her, and his voice was dark with the rough warmth of velvet. 'When you've fallen in love with someone new, and you're trembling on the brink. When you want them to touch you, and hold you. When they kiss you and everything about it is different and exciting—and you want to bury your head in their shoulder, and breathe in the warmth, the smell of them, yet however close you get it isn't enough . . .'

He paused, scouring her face, seeing her eyes and lips weighted languorously by his words.

'You've been there?' he asked her again, but when she nodded a dark shadow like the wing of a moth seemed to pass through the light of his eyes.

'Then you know what it's like——' he said slowly, and his words seemed to take on a drugged reality as he went on '——when you want to devour them, and be devoured by them, and you long to be together, as close as you know how, and yet at the same time you're holding back, wanting the moment never to end . . .'

His voice faded away, as if scorched out of existence by the heat of her beauty looking up at him. He paused, his lips parted, his face tense. Then, before she could even blink, he bent and took her lips with his and a shaft of feeling went through her like piercing lightning.

She was taken completely by surprise, his claiming of her had been so swift and certain. Yet after a second he groaned, a light, quick catch of sound in his throat, as if he too was caught off guard by the feelings he had ignited, and his hands moved up to hold her head up to his and take her lips in a hard but measured kiss that made her open like a lake inside.

It was different, this kiss, from their embrace of the night before. It seemed weighted with poignant desire and genuine longing. Yet as he caught her closer she was moved by his hard strength and purpose, a male arrogance and certainty that her body remembered plainly from his last embrace, and which inflamed her every bit as much as his mouth, exploring hers in an endless fusion of desire.

He pulled back and looked at her, his breath ragged.

'Mandy,' he groaned, and Bella shut her eyes quickly, for fear he was close enough, now, to see the deceit behind her false name. But he read her gesture as submission and caught her closer so that she felt the whole hard length of him, the muscled strength of his body, and his lips claimed hers again in an endless kiss that made her thoughts fragment into a million pieces and her body ache in all its most secret parts for him.

When he finally put her from him, he was breathless and his eyes were lit with dark lights of desire. 'Believe it or not, I didn't mean to do that,' he said shakily. 'It wasn't part of my plan. But I can't say I'm sorry.'

She looked at the floor, ashamed to let him read her eyes in case there were things there that showed how desperately she longed for him.

'It also came from the heart,' he added roughly. 'Pleasure, not work. Although I don't suppose you'll believe that for one moment.'

She was silent, not knowing what to say or think.

He sighed and pushed a hand through his hair. 'Come on,' he said at last. 'To work.'

At once he seemed to snap back into his director's role, pushing her here and there to show her the movements he wanted in the scene, the gestures he envisaged.

She moved like a robot, her body still flooded by the feelings of his kiss, until finally he moved her to the window.

'The last shot will be of you here, looking out through the slats of the blinds. The camera will be on you from behind.' He was behind her. 'I want you to reach up and begin to loosen your sarong, like this.' His hands took hers, moved them for her, showing her the languorous gestures he wanted. She trembled under his touch. 'Don't worry, it'll all be perfectly decent. All the audience will see of you——' he moved her hands, with their handfuls of light cotton, down to her hips '—will be the utterly exquisite line of your back.'

She stood there in silence, quivering at the feeling of his breath on the naked nape of her neck, of his hands on hers, and the certain knowledge that the eroticism of the moment had become real for them both again, and no longer part of the make-believe world of movies.

For a long moment Luke did nothing. She knew she was helplessly in thrall to him. Everything from the hot hum of the cicadas outside the window to the dusky light inside the room seemed pregnant with anticipation. She imagined his hands moving to cup her naked breasts. He was perfectly capable of such a thing, and, if he did it, if he turned her to him and began to make expert love to her, she was not sure she would not have the strength to resist him. She would not even want to.

Slowly, very slowly he dropped his mouth to the soft, downy hairs of her neck, brushing her skin with lips that dragged a little along her skin. She shivered, deeply, at the unbearable sensation, and her body tightened everywhere with wanting. His hands left hers to span the narrow slimness of her ribcage. She heard his breath rasp unevenly near her ear as his tongue gently tasted the salt warmth of her skin.

'Mandy——?' There was a rough question in his voice, but at that very moment the door was pushed open and a man came walking in.

'Whoops! Sorry.' He stopped in his tracks, and turned to go. Luke's lips froze on Bella's skin, then he raised his head calmly.

'It's OK, Keith. It's only work. I'm running through the scene with Mandy.' He let her go. 'Do you want to set up the lights?'

Bella anchored her sarong hastily back into place.

To her heightened senses Luke's lie seemed a flimsy pretence, since the very room still seemed to throb with their abruptly terminated embraces, yet Luke himself looked entirely self-possessed.

'Off you go to make-up,' he instructed her briskly, 'and don't forget to tell them to do your back.'

Yet had it been real? she wondered later, as she prepared for the evening ahead. Or had she simply longed for it to be that way? Luke had said it came from the heart, but that meant nothing. After all, it was plain that, if his heart lay anywhere, it was with his work.

And she had to admit it. The yearning passion of their private embraces in that silent, sultry room had made it all too easy for her to project the kind of restless, roused expectancy that Luke wanted in the scene. It had gone brilliantly, and when she stood at the window and loosed the sarong to her waist she did it with a natural languorous sensuality that was for his eyes alone.

Had he simply worked on her, like a potter working on raw clay? Or had he kissed her because he could not stop himself from taking her in his arms?

'Oh!' She slammed her hairbrush down in an agony of frustration and glowered angrily into the mirror of her dressing-table. In five minutes she had to go out and meet Luke and Guy and Caroline and drive to the neighbouring beach hotel for dinner. She did not want to go, but Luke had organised it, and left her no option.

'Oh!' she groaned again, suddenly longing to be back in her own skin, her own life. But her own skin had changed, she thought. She wasn't the same woman as the restrained Bella Latham of the Institute of Health. The sun had tanned her skin to a light golden colour, and had streaked her hair with natural wheaten strands. She felt more comfortable with her beauty than she had ever done before and had no desire at all to return to the plain Jane she had always struggled to be before.

And there was another problem, too, she admitted honestly to herself. For years now she had lived mainly for her work, shunning relationships, but Luke had made her body stir and wake, and had shown her how much she was missing. The nun's habit she had worn for so long no longer seemed to fit her, and she felt charged with new and restless longings.

The trouble was that now she was no one, she thought bitterly. She certainly was not Mandy Latham, the film star. For, although she understood a little more of what Mandy got out of her chosen profession, she had no desire at all to follow in her footsteps.

But neither was she the Bella she had left behind. She had come to Mauritius as Mandy, and somehow she had managed to lose her own self on the way.

She sighed and reached for her dress, her heart heavy at the prospect of the evening ahead. She did not look forward to hours of fending off Guy's advances. or watching Luke's and Caroline's cosy familiarity.

She bit her lip as she thought about that. Because, when it came to Luke, one thing above all else was certain. Whatever had happened between them in that room this afternoon, however real the tension and desire that had pulled them together, on his part it could be nothing more than a quick fling with yet another beautiful young actress.

Hadn't both Caroline and Guy warned her plainly enough? And, if she was foolish enough to ignore their warnings, she would land herself in very big trouble indeed.

CHAPTER SEVEN

THEY drove south along the coast, with sea breezes blowing through the open sides of their Jeep. Luke had taken the wheel and Caroline had hopped quickly in beside him, leaving Bella and Guy to take the back seat.

Guy lit a cigar and said, 'Lord, it's good to get away. You start to feel human again.'

Caroline laughed, showing flawless teeth and flashing her eyes at Luke. 'It's true, you know. Maybe you should write it into everyone's contract—they should spend at least one evening a week in the real world. It would stop all those molehills turning into mountains.'

'It wouldn't have worked in Scotland, though, would it?' said Luke. 'Or when we were stuck out in the Tunisian desert for four weeks. There would have been nowhere to go. Heavens, do you remember that? All those problems with the drivers, and nothing to eat but camel curry. That was the worst month of my life.'

'And mine,' Caroline said with feeling. 'I handed my notice in halfway through.'

'Did you?' Luke turned with surprise, so that from her seat in the back of the Jeep Bella could see his profile, the warmth in his laughing eyes and crooked mouth. She looked quickly away, jealousy rising in her throat like bile.

'I did. You just didn't bother to open the envelope.' Caroline turned to the back, pointedly directing her remarks towards Guy, ignoring Bella. 'That's typical of him. He knew it was going to interrupt the matter

87

in hand, so he ignored it and hoped it would go away.'

'And it did, didn't it?' Luke teased her. 'Anyway, why do I pay you the vast salary I do, if not to solve my problems for me?'

The easy warmth between them was tangible. Bella did not care one bit that Caroline chose to pretend she did not exist, but this camaraderie made her ache with bitterness and longing.

She frowned and stared hard at the sea, marked by a white line of foam where waves broke gently over the coral reef, until at last they turned into the manicured grounds of the hotel where they were to eat.

Guy marched straight to their terrace table without even glancing at the sumptuous surroundings.

'I don't get the feeling you're much of a sightseer?' Luke teased him as they settled in their chairs.

'Luke, I've been all over the world, and I can honestly say I prefer people to places.' He winked heavily in Bella's direction. 'Although I much prefer some people to others.'

She looked away, straight into Luke's direct glance, and her heart did several somersaults. It was the first time they had looked openly at each other this evening, and their eyes locked with the knowledge of what had passed between them that afternoon. He looked impossibly handsome tonight, with an extra gleam in his compelling eyes that came, she guessed, from the pleasure of a good day's work under his belt, and for a luxurious moment she allowed her eyes to drink him in before looking away.

Luke kept his eyes on hers, although when he spoke it was to Guy. 'That's right, even in Tunisia you hardly left the hotel——'

'No, because I was just about dying from terminal dysentery. A fact you totally refused to acknowledge, you slave-driver. . .'

The talk quickly flowed between the two men and Caroline during dinner. Bella kept very quiet, contributing only in smiles and nods as they swapped stories, and let her eyes dwell surreptitiously on Luke's lean, handsome face as the conversation flowed over her head.

She was just admiring the way his hair curled into his neck below his ear and the play of muscles at his collarbone when he turned towards her.

'But you worked with him once, didn't you?'

'I—sorry, I wasn't——'

'Lou Mecker. He directed you in *Time of the Angels*.'

'I. . .' She floundered like a fish on dry land, caught completely off guard.

'*Time of the Angels*,' he repeated slowly, a frown-line of disbelief marking the space between his brows. 'That television series you were in last year.'

'Oh, yes!' She recovered a little, improvising wildly. 'We always called it *"Angels"*. I didn't recognise its full title for a moment.'

'What's he like then? Does he live up to his reputation?' said Guy.

'I—er—yes. Yes, I suppose he does.'

Luke's eyes did not leave her face.

'Reputation for what?' said Caroline.

Bella took a breath, praying for rescue. It came, but not before Luke had seen the lost look on her face.

'Drink, mainly,' said Guy. 'And temper. I think the two go together.'

'I saw you in that,' Luke said to her. 'You did a good job. In fact, that's when I first started thinking about you for this part. Not that you were all that impressive in the first audition—do you remember?'

She searched her memory for details from Mandy's crib notes.

'I had laryngitis, I could hardly speak.'

'That's right.' He smiled at her and she felt almost giddy with relief. 'I had no idea whether you were any good or not, but I thought it only fair to give you a second chance. Then you turned in a scorcher of a performance.'

She smiled radiantly at him, thinking how happy Mandy would be to hear of his praise.

'You've hardly said a word all night, Mandy.' Luke settled back in his chair. 'Tell us something about yourself. You were at Guildhall, weren't you? You must have been there with Diana Seabrook.'

'I was, but I didn't know her.'

'Surely you were both working in York for a time?'

'We didn't have much to do with each other,' she parried, panic rising up in her chest.

'What was your best part up there?' His eyes were narrowing. She could see he could sense something was not right, but he did not know what it was. Her mind stripped over the lines of Mandy's notes. Thank goodness she had always had a good memory.

'I enjoyed being in *King Lear*—I played Cordelia—even though it was a terrible production. But I never want to be in a pantomime again as long as I live. All those children running up and down and squealing!'

He laughed, his face gentler now, but his probing continued.

'You're a mystery to me, Mandy Latham.'

Bella's eyes opened wide on his. 'Oh? Why is that?'

'You're so quiet, retiring—you seem to resent anyone asking you questions. I'm not used to actresses like you——'

'I hate talking about myself!' she burst out, with such vehemence that everyone jumped. 'I'm just not that interesting. I haven't done anything interesting. I can't tell good stories, and I haven't been anywhere interesting. Not like all of you, with your stories of the Tunisian desert and so on—oh——' To her horror she found tears threatening in her eyes. She turned to Luke. 'You're looking at me as if I've got something to hide, but it isn't a crime just to want to stay quiet and listen!'

'Hey, hey, take it easy.' He reached over and squeezed her arm. 'No one's accusing you of anything.' His fingers were gentle, but his eyes still probed hers sceptically.

'Have another drink, Mandy,' said Guy, refilling her glass, 'and leave her be, Luke. The poor girl's been working her you-know-what off all day.' Bella turned to her saviour, smiling hugely in relief, and, as if he had been waiting for just such an opening, Guy immediately slipped his arm along the back of her chair. Luke's eyes took in the movement and she saw him frown, and something wayward inside her made her lean pointedly back into Guy's embrace. To her satisfaction, the frown deepened, and deepened still further every time she smiled at Guy, or held his gaze in a lingering glance.

Caroline was quick to encourage the new liaison. When they finally left the restaurant, well into the early hours, she ushered Guy and Bella into the back seat of the Jeep with an arch, 'You two love-birds can curl up together in here.' And when, sitting there, Bella felt Guy's arm pulling her close towards him, she was too tired and drained to protest. She must have drunk more than she realised, she thought hazily, because her head was spinning and, although she stared hard at

Luke's dark head in the seat in front, he seemed as remote and distant as a statue carved in granite.

When they pulled up outside their own hotel Guy pointed to the white beach, sparkling in the moonlight, and drawled, 'How can you resist an invitation like that, Mandy? Come for a swim?'

'No, Guy. It's late.'

'Well, a walk, at least. Down to the sea. Just to clear our heads.'

Bella looked across to where Luke and Caroline stood talking close together, Caroline's hand on his arm.

'All right,' she agreed dully, and allowed him to lead her down to the powder-soft sand and the whispering sea.

The beauty of the tropical night tugged at her heart-strings. The sea was calm and marked by a silver path of moonlight, and the sand under her toes was still warm with the day's heat. She remembered how she and Luke had stood barefoot together, his arms about her, and she ached for his touch again. If he were beside her now, she felt she would be able to hold nothing from him.

But it was Guy, cigar-smelling and burly, who tried to draw her closer into his encircling arm. She resisted its pressure.

'I'm going back now,' she said, after they had walked for a time, and turned abruptly.

They walked up the beach and through the palms until they reached her bungalow. She fished in her handbag for her key. Guy took it from her, and as he did so he pulled her into his arms and kissed her.

They had kissed before, on set, but that had been a cosmetic embrace, without substance. Now she felt his seeking lips trying to open hers and his tongue thrusting hard into her mouth.

'Don't——' She thrust him away. 'Please, don't——'

'Come on, Mandy.' He did not loosen his arms, and in the moonlight Bella saw the wet gleam of his eye and realised he was more drunk than she had thought. 'Come on, don't play games with me.'

'I'm not playing games. I just want to go to bed. Let me go.'

'Of course you want to go to bed. *I* want to go to bed. That's why we're here.' He pulled her to him again and placed his lips wetly on hers.

'Don't!' It came out as a half-scream as she struggled in his arms, but wherever her head went his seemed to follow.

'Oh, honey, I know you're hot for me. Look what happened on the set today! That wasn't acting, that was real. You don't have to go through this hard-to-get number.'

'I'm not going through any number! Just get your hands off me!'

'I like a fight,' he said indistinctly, and then they were struggling for real as he pinned her back hard against the wall of her room and began to take her lips in earnest.

'You—you——' Sheer fury made her rake his back with her nails and the pain roused him further.

'Why, you little hellcat,' he muttered. 'I'll have marks there tomorrow. Well, if you like it rough——'

'Oh!' she screamed, as he clawed at her dress. She'd read about stories like this, but could not believe it was happening to her. But she could not muster enough strength to push him away.

Then she saw from the corner of her wild, open eyes a dark running figure. A second later Guy was torn away from her by the collar of his shirt.

'What in hell are you doing?' Luke held him, looked to her. 'What's going on?'

She opened her hands, trembling. The front of her dress was torn, leaving half her breasts exposed. 'He wanted—he was going——'

'You didn't let him expect——?'

'No! Of course not!' she shouted hysterically. 'Why do men always want to blame women?'

'The little bitch is as randy as hell. She's just asking for it. You've seen it, you know what I mean. I know you do—I've seen you two together——'

'Why, you——' said Luke rawly, and hit him squarely on the jaw with a devastating fist. There was a dull crunch of flesh on bone and Guy crumpled up like a dead man.

Luke looked at him dispassionately. Bella gasped, hands pressed to her mouth. 'You've killed him!'

'Of course I haven't. I know how to pull my punches. He's out from drink as much as anything. Give me your key.'

He stepped over Guy's prone body and unlocked the door.

'You can't just leave him there.'

'Why not? He'll hardly be eaten by white ants. They wouldn't like the taste.'

'But shouldn't we get him to bed, or something?'

'When he comes to he'll stumble off into the night, feeling pretty sorry for himself. Guy's OK when he's sober, but he can turn mean when he's drunk. This isn't an entirely new scene for him. I've seen versions of it before.'

She looked at the inert bulk on the floor. She was still shaking. 'It doesn't fit his image though, does it? From his publicity you'd think he could drink anyone under the table.'

Luke gave her a strange, sideways look. 'That's the movies, though, isn't it? That's pretend, not real. Where people like Guy go wrong is mistaking one for the other.'

'And you never do?'

'Never. And I somehow think you don't either. You seem to have your head screwed on pretty firmly.'

She shook her head. 'It doesn't feel like it tonight.'

'Come on, go in.' He ushered her into the room, where she sank exhausted on to the bed. He squatted on his haunches in front of her and carefully moved the torn front of her dress to see her flesh. There were angry red marks at the top of her breasts, which his fingers moved to examine.

She jumped back at the exquisite tenderness of his touch, almost too much to bear after Guy's rough pawings, and he grimaced, looking up into her eyes. 'You've been mauled by one man and now I suppose you think you're being mauled by another.' He sighed, took his fingers from her soft flesh and raked them through his hair.

'No, no, it's not that. It's just that I feel—I don't know—dirty, somehow, and ashamed. As if it were all my fault.'

He smiled. 'That's what you said about men—that they always blamed the woman. Anyway, no one would dream of thinking that about you. And, what's more, no one need know a thing about it.'

'*You* know.'

'Yes, I know.'

'You heard the things he said——'

'Yes, I did.' His voice was quiet, implacable.

'Oh!' It was a sob, and she ran her palm restlessly over the counterpane, feeling the silky material slip under her skin.

'I shouldn't have gone for that walk with him. It gave him ideas.'

'He had them already. He's had his eye on you from the first. Anyway—you didn't exactly freeze him off tonight, did you?'

She blushed, but said, 'It wasn't that. He thought that the way that scene on the beach went this morning was because I fancied him.'

He paused before replying quietly, intently, 'But *we* know differently, don't we?'

She had to look away from his eyes. She got up and paced the room.

Luke got up, too, but did not come near her.

'What do you want to do?' he said in a briskly normal voice. 'Shall I pour you a drink? Or do you just want to be left alone? Guy won't trouble you again.'

'No—no—I don't know——'

She stopped by the window and looked out across the silver beach, then turned impulsively. 'Luke, I want to go out. I want to walk by the sea.' Suddenly it seemed imperative to get back into the balmy night air, to walk and walk until the exquisite perfection of the night calmed her thoughts and restored her senses to order.

But Luke's mouth was set hard and grim.

'I don't think that's a good idea—unless you're planning to go alone. And that probably isn't all that safe . . .' She imagined she heard the word 'either'.

But she needed Luke there, at her side, to wipe out the memory of Guy's horrible pawings at her. As the sea washed clean the beach, so his strong, calm presence would wipe away her tainted memories.

Her open, pleading face brought anger to his face.

'Look, Mandy, face reality! Think what you're asking. I'm not some white knight on a charger riding to your rescue. I might have saved your skin just now, but that doesn't mean I'm some saintly creature without a base thought in my head. And look at that!' With an angry sweep of his hand he indicated the perfect, moon-drenched tropical night. 'Have you ever seen a more romantic setting? Why, it's like something out of a film, a cheap love-film——'

'Don't——' She hated his anger, the dangerous glitter of his eyes.

'I only want you to face the truth.' He came over and stood close in front of her. 'Have you forgotten what happened last night? This afternoon? You know how things are between us, what's been going on——'

She shook her head wildly, 'No, I don't! I don't at all! I can hazard a few guesses, but they don't add up to anything sensible——'

'Oh, come on. How old are you, Mandy? Twenty-three, twenty-four? You're hardly a babe in arms. You're surely acquainted with the simple facts of life by now?'

Her eyes raked his. 'Simple?' she flung back. 'There's nothing simple about you, Luke Retford. You're as devious as any man I've ever met.'

He gripped her arm furiously. 'There are some things so simple that no one can make them complicated. Why won't you hear what I'm telling you? Goodness knows, I'm doing it for your own good—I'm telling you that, if you and I go for a walk in the moonlight, then you'll be walking straight back where you've just come from. I might not be made of exactly the same stuff as Guy de Vere—I hope to goodness I still know that when a woman says no she means it—but my feelings towards you are every bit as primitive.'

Her lips were parted, her eyes were wide, as his

angry torrent of words rained over her. This wasn't the languorous, manipulating Luke she had known before. This was Luke as raw and honest as she had ever seen him, and she felt sure that his anger was directed as much at himself as at her.

Paradoxically, as he faced her so nakedly, she was overwhelmed with the desire to take him in her arms and replace his heated words with heated kisses.

The feeling was so strong that she almost started forward, then she swallowed violently, alarmed at herself. She seemed to be someone else, not herself at all. Maybe she was Mandy? Maybe she had lived her sister's life for so long now that she had begun to behave as Mandy would? After all, Mandy had always had more boyfriends, had lived her life on a series of emotional swings and roundabouts. Yet somehow she had a hunch that Mandy would never have struck the same emotional sparks from Luke that she was causing now.

No, if she was someone else it was another version of herself, the Bella Latham she had buried for so long, that was now bursting through all those long years of denial and repression, and demanding to be free.

Luke was pushing a hand abstractedly through his hair, gazing round the room as if trying to distract himself from her. She followed his eyes and saw them rest in frowning puzzlement on the books and files that she had brought with her in the hope of snatching a few quiet working hours. Suddenly there was an even more imperative reason to get him out of this room.

'I've got to get out!' she cried. 'I feel I'm stifling to death in here. But I'd be scared to go alone. Please come with me.'

His eyes went back to hers.

'Didn't you hear a word I said?' he ground out.

'How can I put it more bluntly? Mandy, I don't want to hurt you, especially not after what you've just gone through tonight. But my intentions towards you are almost entirely dishonourable. *You* might feel like a companionable walk. *I* don't.'

Bella searched his face.

'Hell, Mandy, are you being deliberately obtuse?' he burst out again. 'I'm saying I'm no good as a chivalrous escort; the role doesn't suit me. I'm not a friend in need—I don't feel even the slightest bit friendly towards you! Nothing in the world would give me more pleasure at this moment than walking in the moonlight with you, but I can't promise to keep my hands off you. I can't promise to even try. If we end up walking out of this door together, then as sure as hell we're walking straight into something else.

Bella searched his face for a long time before she replied, but there had never been any doubt about her answer. There was a full moon outside—maybe she was a little mad—but she swallowed and a low, sure voice that hardly seemed her own said, 'In that case, so be it.'

CHAPTER EIGHT

IT WAS strange, but the words which had seemed such a wild declaration to Bella at that moment had thrust Luke away from her. As they walked across the grass and out of the palm trees on to the ghostly white sand he walked beside her, but some way apart, his hands pushed down firmly into the pockets of his jeans.

Jeans, she noticed. Between getting out of the car tonight and running to her rescue he had changed. Probably he'd been getting ready for bed, and had reached for his jeans in haste when he'd heard her screams outside.

'Where's Caroline?' she said abruptly, following an uncomfortable chain of thought.

He gave her a lidded, sideways look. 'In bed, I expect. Sleeping the sleep of the just.'

'Won't she——?' She stopped. She had been going to ask whether she would wonder where he had got to, but it seemed too much of an intrusion into his personal life. He obviously thought so, too, because he chose to walk on as if he had not heard.

'Worry, worry,' he said softly, after a while. 'Look around, there's only us in the whole wide world. Even Guy had gone, did you notice? I expect he slunk off with his tail between his legs at the first opportunity.'

'Poor Guy. It can't be much fun for him, with his marriage breaking up like that.'

'He's had plenty of experience. After all, he's tied the knot six times, and he and Veronica only lasted six months anyway.'

'Oh, I didn't know that.'

He stopped abruptly and wheeled around to face her. 'Mandy, where have you been hiding? Guy's kept the gossip columns in business for the past twenty years.'

'I don't read them.'

'What do you read?' he said swiftly, then answered his own question. 'Thomas Hardy—among a host of other things.'

'How did you know that?'

'I saw it by your bedside table, on top of a considerable pile of bedside reading. I must admit I was surprised.'

'Why should you be?'

'In my experience, most actresses prefer to stick to the latest Hollywood saga novel. They live through their emotions, not their intellect.'

'And what's wrong with that?'

'Nothing. I find it very endearing—at least for a time.' His tone grated on her taut nerves.

'How patronising! I suppose you read Proust every night!'

'It has been known.'

'Lord, you're arrogant, aren't you? Is that why you like directing so much? So you can create a little doll's-house world and look down on everyone in it from a great height?' Why was she talking like this? Was it fear that made her burst out in such tense anger?

'Those are dangerous words,' he said narrowly. 'Maybe I should remind you that *you're* one of my dolls for the time being.'

'I'm nobody's doll!'

'I'll also remind you of something else,' he said angrily. 'You're no great shakes as an actress. Oh, you can do it, if you really try, but you need someone to help you, someone to make you feel the way you have to feel. Right now you need me in order to play this part well. You need me very badly indeed!'

'Oh!' Of course she was no actress! She had never wanted to be an actress! But she could not confess the truth, face him on her own ground. Her hands were tied.

She stormed away along the wavelets, kicking savagely at the spray. What was happening? she thought in furious bewilderment. Why had they flared up at each other the moment they had started talking? Luke walked behind. 'It's me you should be kicking,' he observed after a time, 'not that poor sea.'

She stopped and turned back to him, mastering herself. 'I'm sorry, I know I'm touchy. It's just that everything seems to be going wrong tonight.' The apology was churlish, but at least she managed to get it out.

'Temperamental,' he pronounced, and he smiled as he saw her woebegone looks. 'Actually I quite enjoy your anger. And, look at it this way, if it makes you feel better—you're allowed to be. It's part of being a star.'

'A star? No one's ever called me that before. I've never even felt that way before.'

'And no one's ever said the kind of things you've just said to me before. There's a first time for everything.'

His eyes were on her, making her heart race with nerves, as if there was import in his remark that she could not grasp. He turned and began to walk along the sea's edge. 'Shall I tell you why we're fighting like cat and dog the minute we start talking?'

She glanced at him, her eyes questioning.

'It's perfectly simple. It's because we don't know each other, we don't trust each other—yet we only have to set eyes on each other to set each other alight like the Fire of London. It's a very vulnerable position to be in.' He slanted her a glance. 'It's true, isn't it, Mandy? *You* think I'm just making advances to you to put you in the right frame of mind for the movie. *I* think you——' He stopped, sighing, then burst out, 'I don't know what the hell I think about you! I must say, at the auditions you struck me as the cheerful, robust type. But now you're proving to be altogether more complicated. There's something about you that doesn't add up. All those files and things in your room, for a start——'

'There's no mystery about those!' she cut in fast. 'I'm—very interested in alternative medicine. I'm supposed to be writing a paper about it for my evening class.' Her heart was hammering like an express train.

'But it's not just that. It's something else. As if the real you is always veiled and hidden——'

'I'm sorry if I don't behave the same as all your other young actresses! If I don't read the same books! Only I *do* happen to be an individual!'

'I never for a moment thought you weren't an individual.' Suddenly his hand came out and grabbed her wrist, turning her round to him so fast that her hair flew out and settled in tumbling disarray across her face. 'Stop being so damn defensive! Don't you understand? I'm fascinated by the way you behave. You're like a rainbow dancing in sunlight. Every time I think I've got a fix on you, you dissolve away into opaque white light. You're always hiding yourself, making yourself invisible——'

'Perhaps you're looking for something that isn't there.'

He shook his head slowly, his face very close to hers. 'No, there's something there, something you don't want people to see. But sometimes you can't help it. It shows in your eyes, in the way your mind turns over when you think no one is watching you—the way your mouth broods on secret thoughts.'

Now his voice was dropping to the low sensual husk that she recognised as a thickening with desire. The rough caress of it sent flames licking along her veins.

'I've always thought you were beautiful, Mandy. I've always wanted to make love to you. But now—you're beginning to drive me crazy. I keep thinking about you when I should be thinking about my work. All the schedules are getting quite out of hand.' He smiled a little, self-mocking, rueful. 'The result will be a disaster.'

Bella could feel her face softening, her lips lifting towards him at his words. She shook her head as if to deny what she was feeling 'I—you mustn't. You mustn't feel like that——'

'Why not? You've already said there's no one else.'

'You don't know me.'

'I know I want to know you.'

'You wouldn't like me, if you did,' she said tightly, but his hands were already on her back now, holding her to him.

'Why not?'

Because I'm not Mandy Latham, she wanted to scream. I'm an imposter! I'm boring Bella Latham, with a job that most people think is as dull as ditchwater and a lifestyle to match! And after this week I'll never see you again in my life. And anyway, if you knew the truth about me, you'd be so furious you'd probably throw the kind of right hook at me that you used to knock Guy to the floor earlier this evening.

'Why not?' he insisted again, his eyes very dark on hers.

She forced herself to tear free of him and turn away.

'It doesn't matter. Anyway, perhaps I'm not quite as overwhelmed by you as you'd like to imagine.'

He took her chin and forced her eyes round to meet his. 'You can't fool me with that. What about the "so be it"?' He mocked her earlier bravado with his eyes.

She made her own eyes defiant. 'That didn't mean a thing. After all, you'd already said you wouldn't throw yourself on me.'

He dropped his hand abruptly, holding it tense as if he would slap her. 'Why, you little——! But, on a point of information, that's not what I said. What I said was that when a woman said no I tended to believe her. I haven't heard you say no yet.'

Bella stood unmoving, not speaking, transfixed by him.

'Come on, Mandy,' he taunted her, in a low, desirous voice. 'Can you honestly say you didn't want me to kiss you, last night on the beach?'

He paused. Still she could say nothing.

'Or in the room this afternoon?'

No words came from her dry throat.

'Can you honestly say that you felt nothing when we were alone together then? That, if Keith hadn't come in, nature wouldn't have started to take its course?'

His eyes looked deep into her face.

'And tonight? All that flirtation with Guy—can you tell me that was for his benefit? Or was it for mine?'

Somewhere beyond them the sea whispered over the coral, but the sound came from way off, far beyond their world.

'I haven't heard the word yet,' he taunted her, compelling her with his dark stare and brooding lips.

She struggled with herself, searching for breath, trying to force the single syllable from her lips. But even as she did so he pulled her up to him and stopped her lips with a hot, furious kiss that was like fire to her parched body, igniting her instantly in a flaming need to take her fill of him.

It was over in a second. Luke suddenly stepped

back, pushing her from him, his breath rasping and his eyes dangerous. His chest heaved as if he could not get the air he needed. She touched her mouth with the back of her hand, half expecting it to scorch her skin. She could guess why he had let her go so quickly. The kiss had been an explosion of hot, angry, needing tension. It was too much, too fast, and it had burned him up as much as it had her.

It hadn't been like the other times they had touched. That had always been, in part, a game, she thought in confusion. But this was real, so utterly real that neither of them knew how to handle it.

'We'd better get back. Before I hurl you down here on the sand and do terrible things to you.' The harsh humour did not reach his eyes, which looked at her as though she had struck him.

'Luke . . .' She put out a hand.

'No!' His lips twisted. 'If you won't say the word, I'll be the one to say it. No, Mandy, no. No, no, no! Don't play with fire.'

He set off at a cracking pace back towards the hotel, leaving Bella to hurry after him. After a time she had to run to keep up and her skirt, damp from the spray, tangled around her bare legs, but the gap lengthened and she gave up the struggle. She had a stitch in her side and she bent over, hand on her waist, letting her hair hang down towards the wet sand. She wasn't sure what exactly had happened. All she knew was that Luke suddenly seemed to need to put as much distance between himself and her as he could manage.

She stood like that for a long time, trying to soothe the ache in her side and the ache in her heart. When she straightened she saw Luke had stopped and was looking back to her, waiting. She walked slowly towards him, a slender, waiflike figure in the light of the moon.

'Are you all right?' he said curtly. The anger was still in him; she could see it at a glance.

'A stitch, that's all.'

'Let's get you home.'

They walked in silence through the darkness of the palms to her door.

'Here.'

He took the key. It was a rerun of the same movie, she thought, except that the cast had changed. No, not just the cast, the plot as well. Last time the man had wanted to come in and she wouldn't let him. This time it was all reversed.

'Luke—what happened? What have I done?'

The questions were out before she could stop them. When he saw her pleading look his face slowly untensed from its anger.

'Nothing. It was just one of those things. Go and get your beauty sleep.'

'Don't baby me! I know you're as angry as hell. What I don't know is why! If it's something I've done——'

'Something.' He laughed bitterly. 'No, not something. Everything. Don't you understand? Can't you see how I feel about you? If not, you must be the only person on the set who can't. Ever since you arrived on this island you've been working your way under my skin.' He looked her straight in the eye. 'At first it was easy, just the usual thing. Affairs on film sets are two a penny—why, I could name half a dozen going on tonight around us. I've not been entirely immune from them myself in the past, if I'm honest.

'You see, you were right about the doll's house—in one way at least. Being a director gives you power, and power is one of the most potent aphrodisiacs in the world. It may sound arrogant, but I've come to accept the attentions of young actresses who think I might be able to advance their career as part of the job. When it struck me how much I fancied you, it also struck me how very pleasant it would be to have a brief fling with you in the week while you were here.'

She flushed under his intense gaze, remembering the way she had stood knee-deep in the moonlit sea, letting him see her beauty, and how purposefully he had caught her to him when she had waded back to the shore.

'But, the more I get to know you, then the more impossible that idea becomes. There's something special about you, Mandy, something almost fragile. You're not the type to enjoy a casual affair, are you? Why, I've even found myself wondering if you're a virgin.'

'No, I'm not,' she said quietly, holding his eyes, and thought she saw a ghost of a shadow chase through them. 'I had a boyfriend for years. We were going to get married, but then it finished.'

'And since then?'

She shrugged. 'Nothing, nobody.'

'I can't believe it was for lack of offers.'

'No, there were plenty of offers. I thought I still loved him. It's only since,' she swallowed, 'since I've been here that I've realised that it's really in the past.'

'Why since you've been here?' His eyes burned into her brain.

'Oh, you know why!' She turned her head away sharply, angry at what he was forcing her to reveal. 'Do I have to spell it out?'

He turned her back to face him. 'Because of me?'

'Yes.'

'Oh, Mandy,' there was real pain in his voice, and he raked his hand angrily through his hair, 'what a hell of a muddle! I'm no good for you. We're no good for each other. There are so many obstacles—my work, for one thing. That always comes first——'

'I know all that,' she said sharply, thinking of Caroline. 'Anyone with half a brain can see the obstacles. They're all around, aren't they?'

Their gazes locked for a long moment in a conflict of anger and desire.

'So what you should do is go on inside and shut the door on me and go to sleep.'

'Yes, I should.' Bella was rooted to the spot and her voice was empty of resonance.

'Mandy.'

She looked at him, drinking in his face, the raw honesty in his eyes. I'm crazy about him, she thought. Then, suddenly, piercingly, No, not that. I love him!

His two hands were at her shoulders, but something he read in her eyes at that moment made him drop them sharply to his sides, setting her free. At the open neck of his white shirt, dark hairs curled against his tanned chest. She wanted to throw herself into his arms and feel the rasp of his skin against her cheek. It was like a terrible void inside her that had to be filled.

'Go on in, Mandy, you've got a big schedule tomorrow——'

'We've only got tonight,' she cried wildly, heedlessly. 'It's all we'll ever have!'

'No, Mandy! Don't tempt me.'

'I don't want you to go!'

'I don't want to go. But, Mandy——' his hand sliced through the air '——if I walk through this door with you we'll end up in bed. If we end up in bed, we'll make love. Then tomorrow you leave. Is that what you really want?'

Bella hesitated, searching his eyes.

'I can't offer you anything else. It might work out for us later, it might not. No one knows, but I'm not going to pretend otherwise. You're worth far more than empty promises——'

'And the work comes first,' she said bitterly, thinking of Caroline.

'It's my life.'

'Oh!' She groaned, and his eyes showed pain.

'Do you *want* me to hurt you?' he cried angrily. 'Because that's what will happen.'

She looked at him, and suddenly her own anger flared in response.

'Maybe you're hurting me already! After all, you didn't have these scruples earlier, did you? Not when it suited your own purposes. What about what happened on the beach last night? And this afternoon?'

He dashed his hand through his hair. 'I'm trying to behave decently——'

'Isn't it a bit late for that?'

'Is that what you think?'

They stood close together, breathing hard, lost in their anger and need. He was right, of course he was, and yet she could not bear to let him walk away.

She lowered her head, then tossed her hair back, looking up at him, all the tumult of her heated emotions showing in her face, and she heard him take a sharp breath at the sight of her beauty.

'Mandy, what do you want?' he said, in agony.

'Why do you even have to ask?'

He shook his head, as if to free his thoughts. He was all shadows and darkness, his deep gaze and brooding mouth.

'You don't want this.'

Tears were welling in Bella's eyes, clumping her lashes.

'All I want,' she said brokenly, 'is for you to kiss me.'

CHAPTER NINE

'OH, MY goodness!' Mandy clapped her hand to her mouth in horror. 'You mean you had an affair with him! You had an affair with Luke Retford! I don't believe I'm hearing this.'

'Wait,' said Bella, 'I haven't finished yet.' She looked down, miserably running her fingers over the cotton candlewick bedspread. In Mauritius the cover of her bed had been silky satin beneath her skin. She shut her eyes tight against the worst of the memories. 'I would have done, Mandy, I can't pretend otherwise. But in the end I didn't.'

'Why, what happened?'

'Caroline happened.'

'Oh.' Mandy whistled long under her breath. 'The ice queen.'

Bella kept her eyes shut. When she had decided she had to tell Mandy everything, she had had no idea it would be so painful. They had been talking for hours, ever since her plane had arrived in London that morning, and she still had not reached the most difficult part.

'Hold on,' said Mandy, looking at her sister's bent head. 'I'll make some more coffee.'

Alone, Bella let the exquisite, bitter memories flood in. Luke's iron will had been broken by her plea. He had kissed her when she'd asked him to, not with the angry wanting she'd expected, but with a slow, controlled yearning that had caught her so off guard that it had flooded her instantly with melting desire. Every atom of her had dissolved with a longing that

had curved her at once into his arms and opened her
lips beneath his, so that he would not take her mouth
from hers, but had searched it harder, deeper, more
insistently.

His warmth and strength had been a drug her body
craved and she had yielded against the length of him,
so that the desire he had penned back had flared
quickly to a hardening need that had made his lips
rough against hers and sent shudders of delight to the
deepest parts of her.

He had moved his hands restlessly to her throat, to
the soft skin of her neck beneath her hair, to her bare
arms. The seeking pressure had been exquisite. It had
made her gasp with pleasure and push her hands into
his hair so she could hold his lips down to hers.

She'd felt lost, abandoned in love, and her mood had
ignited him. 'Mandy,' he'd groaned, 'what you do to
me——' But he had not been able to finish his sentence,
only to bury his head against the warmth of her skin.

Some time later, she could not remember when in
their long, tumultuous discovery of each other, he had
raised his head and looked at her, his eyes lit with
warmth, the skin along his cheekbones flushed, his
mouth brooding with desire, and he had asked her,
simply, 'Mandy?'

The false name had arrowed her heart with pain, and
she had lowered her forehead to his shoulder to hide
her deceiving eyes, but he had mistaken her gesture
and tipped her chin to search her eyes for doubt.

'I'll go if you tell me to,' he got out. 'I'm not Guy.
Only for heaven's sake tell me now, not later.'

But the look of him, the strength of him against her
had sapped her senses. In answer her lips had opened
against his collarbone and he had groaned and stirred
and caught her up to him again.

'So what happened?' Mandy repeated, handing Bella a steaming mug. 'How far did you go? Oh, lord,' she raised her eyes to the ceiling, 'how far did *I* go?'

The sisters looked at each other in despair. 'I didn't mean to, Mandy. Honestly I didn't,' Bella pleaded wretchedly. 'I don't know what came over me.'

'Luke Retford came over you,' Mandy answered tartly. 'He comes over very strong. He has a reputation for it.'

'Yes,' Bella said painfully. She doodled with her finger on the bedspread. He had been strong. Every bone and muscle of him had pulsed with a raw male energy she had never known before. Yet, even in their passion, his hands had been gentle, rousing. She swallowed at the memory of his palm running restlessly up under the flimsy skirt of her dress and his murmured marvellings at the length of her slender legs. 'It was clear he was no novice,' she said abruptly.

Mandy's look softened. 'Oh, love, I'm sorry—if I'd known you'd get hurt like this——'

'If we'd both known the half of it, we'd never have embarked on such a damn fool scheme! But it's a bit late now.'

They sipped their coffee in silence for a moment. Then Mandy said, 'Tell me the worst and get it over with.'

Bella took a heavy breath and said in a wooden voice, 'We got into my room together, we ended up on the bed. We still had most of our clothes on when we were so rudely interrupted.'

'Most?' Mandy enquired tentatively. 'It doesn't sound *too* disastrous.'

'I had my dress unbuttoned. He had his shirt half off.'

'And that's all?' Mandy was looking distinctly

relieved.

'That's all.' Only how could she ever tell Mandy how it had felt when they had been together like that? As if they were drowning in each other. As if they were destined to fuse into one single being. Even Luke, with all his doubtless experience, had felt something, she was sure. His eyes had looked into hers as if he would know her very spirit, and his hands had cupped her face with wonder. And when that cruel, peremptory knock at the door had broken the moment it had felt as if the very world had stopped turning.

Luke had raised his head, his hand still cupping her warm breast, then nodded at her.

'Yes, who is it?' she had called.

'It's Caroline. I'm looking for Luke,' the voice had rapped out, cold and hard. Bella's mouth had gone dry. Luke had thrown himself back with a curse on the bed, leaving her cold and alone. She had not known what to do. She had looked at him. He had called out, harshly, 'What is it, Caroline, that can't wait until the morning?'

'It's New York on the phone—as you would know, if you slept in your own bed. Howard Mills wants to speak to you urgently. He's hanging on while I find you.'

With a curse, Luke had got up, kissed Bella swiftly on the mouth and headed for the door. He had been buttoning his shirt as he'd left. Caroline's eyes had darted instantly to the rumpled bed and Bella's own disarrayed figure on it, and she had shot her a look of pure hatred before the door had closed behind them both.

'And that's all?' Mandy said.

'Isn't it enough?' Bella sighed heavily. 'My last day was no joke, as you can imagine.'

'What, with Guy and everything?'

'Guy was the least of my problems. He apologised pretty effusively, but he didn't seem particularly abashed. I even wondered if he could remember exactly what he'd been up to. And it wasn't as difficult seeing Luke again as I thought it was going to be. I dreaded having to face him, but when he's directing he obviously thinks about nothing else.'

That was a flexible account of the truth. In fact, it had been horribly painful to have to see him again, and to realise just how little their involvement seemed to have impinged on his life. And even worse had been having to act out with Guy, under Luke's critical gaze, the kind of passion she had known for real in her room the night before. Yet, as they had worked on this final scene, his eyes had been hard, his mouth set and his directions so brusque that no one would ever have guessed what had taken place between the two of them less than twelve hours before.

No one except Caroline, of course. 'It was Caroline,' Bella confessed. 'She sought me out and gave me the works.'

'What sort of works?'

Bella grimaced, remembering the jealous woman's icy eyes and splintering words. 'What it amounted to was a half-hour tirade about steering clear of Luke, and not getting fancy ideas about myself and him because he had any number of flings with two-bit actresses like myself, while she, Caroline, was a permanent feature on the scene, and had been for years.'

'Ugh. Nasty.'

'Very. Although I think I kept my end up. I seem to remember telling her that *I* wouldn't stand for a man who played around like that, and that if she wanted other women to steer clear she ought to get him to advertise their relationship a bit more prominently.' Bella sighed heavily. 'A little part of me even felt a bit sorry for her. She obviously has a lousy time.'

'With a heel like Retford, you mean?'

'Exactly. He's really got it taped, hasn't he? Home comforts when he needs them, but no ties.' Bella stared bleakly round the bedroom. 'I left him a "Dear John" note. Thanks, but no thanks. I went on about it all being a mistake, and how it would be better for everyone if we resumed a strictly professional relationship next time we met—so at least you can turn up in Wales pretending it never happened.'

Mandy pulled a despairing face. 'I'll have to, won't I? But I can't say I look forward to it. If he's got that close up to you, he's bound to see the difference. I'll never get away with it.'

'You'll have to try. There's no way I'm going near a film set ever again.' But Bella exchanged a doubtful look with Mandy. 'He may, anyway. See the difference. I had no idea how personal a thing acting is. You're reaching down inside yourself all the time and pulling out your private emotions. . .' Her voice tailed away as she thought of all she had remembered and felt during the last week. For the first time in years she had confronted her memories of Nick and laid his ghost. And that had left her free to dig down inside herself and discover the person she now was.

The only trouble was that that person was no longer the controlled and single-minded Bella Latham of the Institute of Heath, but a new woman whose passions had been stirred and whose needs had been left naked and exposed. She looked up at Mandy, then despairingly round the small bedroom of their London flat, and her sister, seeing her look, exclaimed under her breath and jumped up to hug her.

'Oh, Bell, I'm so sorry it's been like that for you!'

Bella blinked back sudden pricking tears of tiredness and emotion. 'And I'm sorry I've made such a mess of everything for you.'

Mandy hugged her harder. 'Don't say that. You haven't made a mess, at all. Good heavens, I can't think of anyone I know who'd resist a pass from Luke Retford.'

A pass. Bella's heart sank like lead to hear it put so baldly. Because, of course, that was what it had been. A pass and nothing more. A straightforward, run-of-the-mill pass at—what was it Caroline had called her?—'a two-bit actress' like all the other two-bit actresses he had known. And the fact that when he had taken her in his arms it had felt as if all the moons and the stars in the universe were exploding in her head made not the slightest bit of difference to the way things really had been between them.

She lifted her head and managed a rueful, grim-faced grin at her sister. 'Well, take my advice, if the situation should rear its ugly head again—have a jolly good try!'

CHAPTER TEN

A MONTH later Mandy, spot-free and quite recovered, packed her suitcase and headed off for Wales to join the last week of filming.

Bella hugged her. 'Good luck.'

Mandy grimaced. 'Last time it was you going off with a sheaf of crib notes, now it's me.'

Bella smiled tightly. 'Shall I test you? What was Guy's favourite drink at the hotel bar?'

'Pina colada.'

'Describe the colour of the sea by the hotel.'

'Er—brilliant turquoise shading to a sort of green with white foam by the coral reef.'

'What was the name of the Chinese restaurant you went to in Port Louis?'

'The Hu Nang.' Mandy's smile faded. 'I'm scared, Bell. It seemed such a simple idea at the beginning, but when you realise how many things can go wrong——'

'Like my falling for Luke, you mean?'

'I'm dreading seeing him. I'm dreading everything. It's going to be far harder acting off-screen than on.'

'Well, it's only for a few days. And I'm sure, if *I* managed, then you'll have no problems. After all, you're the professional actress.' Bella tried to bolster Mandy's failing courage with reassuring smiles, but the smiles did not reach her eyes.

Ever since she had returned from Mauritius, life had seemed dull to the point of screaming, and empty as a void. And, although she and Mandy had agreed that Mandy would handle the problem of Luke by consigning past events to history and refusing to discuss them or even to refer to them, she was tortured by the thought that what had flamed up between her and him would be re-ignited between Luke and her look-alike sister.

She went off to the institute after putting Mandy on the train, and buried her head in a mound of paperwork. The Bristol conference at which she was due to present the work she and her partner, Pete, had done over the past two years was looming. It was a major milestone in her professional life, but she had the utmost trouble in concentrating on what she had to do.

That night she went to the cinema, to see one of Luke's earlier films. It was a war film, about jungle war in Malaysia, not at all her usual sort of choice, and yet she was gripped by the artistry of his filming and moved by the compassion with which the story unfolded. For the first time she began to realise just how talented he was, and how much he must know of human nature to be able to make such powerful films.

The next day she forced herself back to work, even though it was a struggle to discipline her concentration. Yet by the end of the morning, in the quiet of the empty building, she managed to immerse herself so thoroughly that the telephone rang ten times before she got up to answer it.

'Research office,' she said, still frowning at the figures on her computer screen.

'Bella it didn't work—not even for a moment——' Mandy's miserable voice came on the line, only to be cut off instantly by Luke.

'Bella? I gather that's what I should be calling you! I've only got one thing to say. You get yourself here just as quick as you can.' His voice grated with fury, and she sensed he was in such a white heat of rage that he did not trust himself to say more.

She felt sick.

'What——?'

'You heard. I want you here. On set. Preferably today.'

'I can't. Don't be ridiculous.'

'You can—and will.'

Fear made her aggressive. 'I won't. I'm a busy woman. I'm right in the middle of a complicated computer run, and I'm due to speak at a conference tomorrow.'

'Where?'

'At Bristol University.'

'That's the right direction. Pack a case.' The phone went dead.

Bella stubbornly refused to do what he said, but carried only her normal briefcase when she caught the train the next day. In her high-necked white blouse and the expensive charcoal suit she had bought especially for the occasion, she felt a different person from the sun-baked sylph of Mauritius, and her thoughts were coolly defiant. Let him be angry, she thought, there was nothing he could do. After all, all she had done was to help out Mandy.

As for Mandy . . . She frowned when she thought about her sister on the spot to receive the brunt of Luke's rage, but there were limits to what she could do for her. Especially when she had her own immediate worries and fears about the conference to deal with. When today was over, she would turn her thoughts to Mandy's problems.

Anyway, she thought, looking around the conference-room, in this quiet, academic world Luke and his films hardly seemed real. *This* was her world, where she felt happy and at home, and as she listened attentively to the latest findings in her field from Australia and West Germany she even managed to push him from her mind altogether.

Then it was her turn to speak. She had addressed audiences once or twice before, but always nervously, and she felt the same fluttering in her stomach as she walked down the aisle to take the rostrum. But suddenly, as she looked down at the sea of faces turned her way, everything felt different. The paper she was presenting was the distillation of two exciting years' work, and she knew it would attract interest. And somehow, as she looked around and began, with a smile, to speak, she found that her time in Mauritius had taught her more than she had realised about how to project her voice forcefully and calmly.

Her eyes went over the room, noting as she spoke that the ranks of sober-suited men kept their eyes glued to her. She tossed back her sun-streaked hair and allowed her lavender eyes to rest here and there, enjoying the admiration that was coming her way because she knew that it was not based on her looks alone, but on the solid achievement of her work.

And Luke could go to hell, she thought defiantly as she concluded her delivery on a high note of ringing declaration about the future direction of her work, and stood waiting to field the clamour of questions she knew would come.

There was considerable applause, then a brief pause as the chairman selected the first questioner, and in that second she saw a stir of movement at the back by the door. She blinked. She couldn't be sure, but for one extraordinary moment that dark-suited man had looked like Luke.

Afterwards the meeting broke for tea. A colleague

from one of the London teaching hospitals cornered
her. He was a young man with hopeful eyes and a ready
offer of a lift back to London in his car, but just as she
hesitated a dark figure cut through their conversation.

'I'm sorry, but Miss Latham has a prior
appointment.'

She whipped around, angrily. 'You! How dare you
come in here? This is a private meeting.'

Luke was more than angry, he was dark with
repressed fury.

'How dare you risk wrecking my entire movie with
your cheap little trick? Where's your case?'

'I haven't got one. I'm going back to London
tonight.'

'That's right, with me,' the young man chipped in.
'And I don't somehow think Bella wants to talk to
you——'

She felt sorry for him even as he tried to defend her,
and shut her eyes, remembering Luke's right hook
closing on Guy's jaw. But there was no sound of flesh
on bone, only the gentle chinking of teacups and quiet
murmur of conversation all around. She opened them
again.

'*Bella*,' he repeated the word with sarcastic
emphasis, reminding her how often he had called her
Mandy, 'has no option.'

'Don't be ridiculous. I'm in the middle of a
meeting——'

'No, you're not. I've checked the programme. It's
all over—bar the swilling at the trough.' He nodded at
the cups and biscuits.

'There are people I need to see!'

'And there are scenes I need to shoot!'

'That's nothing to do with me!'

'That's everything to do with you! If you start a job,

you finish it!'

'Huh, that's fine coming from you!' The raw innuendo was out before she realised she was going to say it. He knew what she meant instantly, and it set a pulse of rage ticking at his jaw.

He gripped her arm and spoke rapidly, through gritted teeth. 'I'll gladly finish that job, and without the slightest compunction, if that's the price I have to pay to get you to Wales.'

'Don't be so vile! I wouldn't want you near me any more. Let go of me.'

'Not likely, not until you agree to come with me.'

She looked around. Luke's whitened knuckles on her upper arm, their raised voices were attracting attention. Faces were turning towards them. This was her world, she thought furiously, possessively, where she was working hard to make her mark as a serious researcher. And now he was wrecking it all, with his crude Hollywood-style confrontations.

'I'll join you in a minute,' she muttered, 'if you'll only let go of me and let me get out of here with some dignity.'

'You think I'd fall for that? You'll be scuttling out of a side entrance before I can turn round.'

She looked at him coldly and levelly. 'How ridiculous. You've obviously lived in your lurid film world for far too long. Why on earth should I want to do that? I'm not that frightened of you.'

'No? Well perhaps you should be,' he said dangerously, but after a moment he turned on his heel and left.

She smoothed her sweating palms down her skirt and walked over to her conference hosts with her head held as high as she could manage.

The chairman put out his hand. 'My dear, a most

stimulating contribution. Do you know Philippa Edwards, Dr Edwards, from Glasgow? She has been very keen to discuss your findings.'

Bella smiled distractedly at the older woman. 'Perhaps we could talk on the telephone some time soon, only I'm afraid something's come up and I have to leave rather sooner that I expected. You can always get through to me on the institute's main number.'

'Of course.' The older woman smiled, then lifted a humorous eyebrow and said, with surprising roguishness, 'I must say the "something" looks well worth leaving for. You go off with a clear conscience, my girl—you've made far more of a contribution today than most of these stuffed shirts here.'

Bella walked proudly through the throng, a slight and beautiful figure in her tailored suit, and was sustained by the many admiring glances turned her way until she went through the door. But outside, in the entrance, the only look she met was Luke's dark scowl.

'The car's outside.' He took her arm roughly.

'I've told you I'm not going!' She tore her arm away. 'How dare you create a scene like that in front of all those people? Why, half of them are in the position to offer me jobs in the future. Yet you made me look a complete idiot!'

'Perhaps that's what you are. Only an idiot would have thought she could get away with the trick you tried to pull.'

'It wasn't meant to be a trick, only a substitution. You have stand-ins, don't you, in some scenes? What's the difference?'

He squared up in front of her, harsh and dark and powerful, rapping out his words. 'The difference is this. You and Mandy might look alike, but you don't sound alike, you don't feel alike, you don't smell alike. You put out completely different vibrations. If I used you both in this movie the audience would see the join at a glance. And, since we can't go back and reshoot in Mauritius, you'd better come along to Wales and finish your sister's work for her.'

His words were like blows, raining down, stunning her.

'I can't! Mandy's better now. *She's* the actress, it's her part. That was why I did it——'

'Mandy knows the score. She's had a hefty chunk of my views on the whole affair and has run off back to London to lick her wounds.'

Bella thought of Mandy and the rough edge of Luke's tongue, and her heart contracted for her poor twin.

'You beast! Can't you see why she did it? It was the biggest thing that had ever happened to her, and then she thought she was going to lose it all——'

'Well, she has, hasn't she?'

'What do you mean?'

'She'll hardly land another job once this gets out.'

'You mean once you tell everyone!'

'I mean once everyone sees it's another name on the credits.'

'Oh, no—you couldn't do that——'

'I can and I will.'

'What about the unions? They'll kick up trouble. I haven't got a card.'

'That'll be my problem.'

She glared at him, hate pounding along her veins.

'I won't do it!'

'You damn well will! If you think I'm going to see half a million pounds go down the drain, along with a year's work, just because some small-time actress decides to mess me about——'

'You can't make me! I'm going to the cloakroom to get my coat, and then I'm going to catch my train. You try and stop me.'

In a flash he had pushed her against the wall and had his hands each side of her head. 'Just watch me,' he muttered and bent his head to punish her with a furious, painful kiss. 'There, as far as anyone here is concerned we're simply a pair of squabbling lovers. Now let's get your things.' He was far too powerful for her as he marched her across to the cloakroom, his arm hard round her shoulders, and then out towards the car park.

He unlocked the door on the passenger side, still holding her tightly.

'Get in.'

'No!'

'Right.' In a fury he lifted her up and threw her hard down into the seat of the black estate car, then bent to fasten her seatbelt.

He slid into his own seat, eyes glittering.

'Now listen to me, and listen hard. If you refuse to do these scenes, there'll be nothing in it for anyone. Not me, not you, not Mandy. The whole movie will just go down the tube—but I'm willing to do a deal with you. Finish playing the role, and I'll put Mandy's name on the credits and no one need be any the wiser.'

Bella looked at him scornfully. 'I thought you said we were so different, everyone could tell——'

'There'll be rumours, and gossip. There always are in the movie world. But they'll die away soon enough if we all keep quiet. And you're alike enough to people who don't get close to you. It's not your looks that are the problem, it's your vibrations.'

'How can I trust you?'

He reached forward and switched on the engine, taking her words as consent. 'You can't. There's no way. You just have to hope.'

The car sped fast over the Severn Bridge and up into the hills of Wales. Luke drove furiously as if trying to purge his soul of rage. He was a proud man, and not one to fool, Bella thought, and realised what innocents she and Mandy had been when they had embarked on their simple plot.

'Ah!' She gasped in terror as they spun fast round bends. 'You're driving like a madman.'

'I'm perfectly in control.' But he slowed his furious pace.

'I doubt that.'

He flashed her a look.

'Don't goad me further, Bella. I'm in no mood for it.'

'How do you think I feel? Being carted off into the night like this without as much as a toothbrush!'

'I don't give a damn how you feel. And anyway, it's your own fault. I told you to pack a case.'

'And you always expect people to do what you say,' she said bitterly. 'It's the doll's house again, isn't it, and we're just the little figures you move around to suit your grand design?'

'I make movies,' he said. 'I like to do a good job. Just as you do.'

Something in his tone made her flash a surprised look at him, a dark, even profile against the window of the car.

'I saw you deliver your paper,' he said, meeting her glance. 'I was in the back of the hall. I didn't understand more than about half of it, but I *did* understand that your audience was impressed. Although,' she saw his mouth crook a fraction, 'I don't think their rapt attention was *entirely* to do with the soundness of your paper statistics—you cut a pretty glamorous figure up there on the platform.'

She thought about the applause she had received, and then about the quivering excitement she felt at being with Luke again. And suddenly her anger seemed to switch gears and change into a strange, charged excitement at the developments of the day.

Dusk was coming, not the sensuous, sultry dusk of a tropical island, but rather a slow, thick gathering of darkness that turned the mountains to black, brooding sentinels all around. Yet in the car, with Luke, Bella almost began to enjoy the speeding journey through the wild uplands.

'They *were* impressed,' she said, with satisfaction, almost to herself. 'They should be. Pete and I got far better results than we ever hoped for when we set out. I wish he were here to share the glory, but he's spending the summer in the States.'

'Pete?' he quizzed sharply.

'My co-worker.'

He slanted her a glance. 'I don't know anything about you, at all do I?'

She shook her head.

'You must have been laughing up your sleeve in Mauritius, thinking what a fool you were making of us all.' The anger was back in his tone.

'No!' She shot up in her seat, shaking her head vehemently. 'All I felt on Mauritius was sheer terror. I was certain I wouldn't be able to do the job, and I hated being there. I felt such a charlatan!'

'That was because you were.' His anger bit into his words.

'I know.' She turned to him. 'But I only did it for Mandy's sake. Don't you see? She'd worked so hard, and for so long, and she'd had so many disappointments and set-backs. When she landed this job she was just radiant with joy. I couldn't bear her to lose all that. I didn't want to trick anyone, but she said you'd never delay the schedule, or offer her another part.'

His swift glance took in the open pleading of her face, but refused to soften.

'She's right about the first, it wouldn't have been possible. I don't know about the second. She's got talent.'

'She'd have made a far better Dee than me.'

'Not necessarily. She would have played it differently, but your portrayal of her has a whole raw honesty that a professional actress might never have captured. The Mauritian rushes are first rate. I was thrilled to bits when I sat down and ran them all through together. That's why you have to do these last scenes. I need to keep that feeling all the way through, or else the whole thing will fall apart.'

'Would you think about auditioning Mandy for some of your future movies?' she ventured, but his reply was curt.

'I don't know. I'm far too furious with you both to think about anything like that at the moment.'

'Oh!' She exploded with sudden exasperation at his self-centred arrogance. 'It's her *life*! She'll die of disappointment if she doesn't make it—don't you see?'

'I see only too well. You don't have to lecture me on how desperately people in my business want to get on. Contrary to what you might think, I don't actually enjoy turning people down for parts. I hate the whole business of casting more that anything else I do. But everyone who goes into this field has to know that the odds are that they'll fail.'

'I can't imagine you ever thinking you'll fail at anything,' she said bitterly.

His eyes were hard as he drove his foot down steadily on the accelerator once again, but he glanced at her quickly before adding enigmatically, 'It's certainly not a feeling I'm familiar with—I just hope I'm not about to get a closer acquaintance.'

CHAPTER ELEVEN

THEY sped on through the night, silence descending around them like the thick darkness that gathered over the hills. From time to time Bella glanced at Luke, seeing his brooding profile and wondering what thoughts were chasing through his ever-turning mind. They were total strangers to each other, she thought, inhabiting worlds so different they could be living on separate planets, and for some reason the thought made her feel as gloomy as the night that closed in around their speeding car.

'Hey!' She gasped out loud. Although Luke was a good driver, the speed at which walls of solid rock seemed to loom out at them from the night frightened her.

'If it weren't for you, I wouldn't be wasting a day trekking down to Bristol and back! I've no intention of turning the journey into a scenic saunter.'

'If you carry on like this, you'll be wasting far more than a day—you'll be wasting a couple of lives!'

'Don't be ridiculous. I'm perfectly in control.'

'I'll have to take your word for it, because your driving doesn't show any evidence of it!' Her nerves were beginning to twang like overstretched piano wire as the strains of the day took their toll.

He took his foot off the accelerator and looked at her angrily. 'You think you could do better? No? Then kindly keep your back-seat driving comments to yourself!'

He revved up again and she fought to control herself, although her right foot pushed down hard on an imaginary brake each time they turned a bend.

'I suppose time isn't exactly of the essence in your world?' he said pointedly, after a spell of silence.

'And just what is that supposed to mean?'

'All those long-term studies and longitudinal samples——'

'Try telling that to the people who are dying from stomach cancer or heart disease! I strongly suspect they'd like some answers pretty quickly!' she said with asperity, and had the small satisfaction of seeing him nod a little in acknowledgement of his error.

'While I suppose, in your book, I just make movies about made-up stories and fantasy worlds which have absolutely no bearing on the real issues of the day?' With strange insight he voiced exactly the kind of criticisms with which, over the past weeks in London, she had tried to armour herself against her constant thoughts of him.

'I did think that at first,' she admitted grudgingly, 'but then I went to see your film about Malaya. I found it very moving. And very thought-provoking.'

He jerked his head round, surprised. 'Thank you. That's the best thing anyone could ever say about one of my films. I don't claim to have any answers, but I certainly hope to make people think. You see,' he flashed her another glinting glance in the darkness, 'we aren't so very different after all, Bella. You work to try and save lives, I work to try and improve the quality of the lives being lived, by making people think about what they value and stand for.'

A prickle crept along her skin.It was uncanny, as if he had read her earlier thoughts, and had now decided to answer them. But she only said, combatively, 'Most people watch movies just for entertainment—on Saturday night, after a hard week——'

'Then why not entertain and try to educate at the same time?'

'Mmm.'

'This movie we're making now, it isn't simply about a burnt-out cop trying to nail a drug-smuggling ring, it's about innocence and corruption, about personal salvation——'

'I know that, I realised all that in Mauritius. But,' she shook her head, 'I don't know. I guess I simply prefer dealing with concrete facts, the world in front of me. All the pretence and posturing of the movie world doesn't suit me one bit.'

'You're certainly different,' he said slowly, and suddenly there was a dangerous edge in his voice again, 'and of course you never posture, do you, Bella? You'd never dream of pretending?'

'I never do it willingly!'

'But you still manage to do it to devastating effect! You managed to fool us all——and now look at the mess we're in.'

He drove down still harder on the accelerator as his anger mounted again, and once more the bends began to spin alarmingly by.

'Did you ever stop to think——?' he began to exclaim, but she cut him off furiously.

'I only thought about Mandy! She's my sister, for heaven's sake! My twin! You can't expect me to have thought about the film when I didn't know the foggiest thing about movie-making!'

'As was blindingly obvious on that first day in Mauritius! Why I ever persisted with you, I'll never know.'

'You said I was good.'

'You were good. You were devastating. But at what price? I'm beginning to wonder now.'

'I'm here, aren't I? I'm doing what you want. You'll get your film.'

'I will if you can sustain the same performance in the foggy wilds of Wales as you pulled out of the bag in steamy Mauritius. But that's a very big if indeed! After all, you haven't got any training or experience to fall back on, have you? You might be up to your ears in science degrees, for all I know, but that won't count for much under the arc lights, will it? And what you're going to have to do here is a hundred times more demanding than lounging around in a bikini looking sexy in Mauritius.'

'I did it before; I can do it again!'

'I admire your confidence in yourself, but I don't share it. We'll have to see, won't we?'

There was a branch lying on the road. He skidded round it with a squeal of brakes, straightening up fast. 'When I think about the lies that tripped off your tongue out there——' He banged the steering-wheel with his hand '"I'm very interested in alternative medicine. I'm supposed to be writing a paper about it for my evening class." Some evening class!'

'Well, what should I have done? I was there, wasn't I, for better or for worse? I had to keep up the act.' Bitterly she remembered their moonlit walk along the sand. 'I should have stuck to the plan,' she said, and the bitterness was clear in her voice.

'What plan?'

'Well, it certainly didn't include being half raped by Guy de Vere, or—or. . .' She faltered.

'Or by Luke Retford?' he finished caustically. 'Come on, Bella. Surely your objective little scientific brain can't have falsified the data to that extent?'

She flushed, glad of the covering darkness. 'That wasn't what I was going to say! I was going to say, or getting involved with anyone—however casually.'

His eyes slanted towards her, but it was too dark to read his expression.

'Those sort of plans always work better on paper than in real life,' he snapped coolly. 'They leave out the human element.'

'And I should have left out the "human element". I should have just done my work, then gone back to my room. That was what we agreed!'

'You make it sound like a wartime operation. Did you have crib sheets and briefing notes, as well?'

'Yes! Yes, if you must know, we did! *And* I had my hair cut to look like Mandy's, *and* she gave me acting lessons, *and* I took all Mandy's clothes with me to Mauritius—not because we were scheming harridans, but because we wanted it to work!'

'Which it never could have done in a million years! I'm amazed you could have even thought it might! Goodness, what's that——?' An owl suddenly swooped down low towards their car out of the night, a pale and ghostly shape filling the windscreen. Luke wrenched at the wheel to get away from it, and the car bumped and lurched over the rough ground at the edge of the road, tearing against a rock as he fought to regain the tarmac. They were back on the road almost immediately, but the car lurched pitifully. Luke slammed on the brakes and got out. She heard him kick a tyre and curse vehemently. She got out too.

'What is it?'

'Tyre's torn. Look at it.' He opened the back of the car and wrenched up the floor cover. Then he swore far more violently than before. 'That wretched John Leigh. I'll kill him!'

Bella went to look. There was a gapingly empty space where the spare wheel should have been.

'One of my assistants borrowed the car last week. He told me he'd had a puncture, and that he was getting it seen to. What he didn't tell me was that he hadn't bothered to put the wheel back in the car! I'll kill him when I get my hands on him!'

She looked around and there was nothing to be seen, nothing to be heard, just darkness all around them. Slowly the situation began to sink in. Somewhere nearby an owl—probably the same owl, she thought—hooted long and low. She shivered and folded her arms tightly across her chest.

'What can we do?'

'Wait. There's nothing else we can do. That tyre's beyond repair.'

'But we haven't seen another car for hours!'

'Nor are we likely to. This is well off the beaten track.'

'There must be a town or something!'

He laughed savagely. 'There speaks a city girl. I think there are a couple of villages, but not for miles.' His mouth twisted. 'In the morning, if we're very, very lucky, the occasional van or tractor might pass this way.'

'The morning?'

He raised his head and looked at the sky, pushing a hand through his hair.

'The morning. So we finally get to spend the night together after all, Bella.'

'Stop it!' She could not bear the cold dislike in his voice. 'It isn't *my* fault you've ripped open one of your tyres. You should have driven more slowly.'

'If it weren't for you, I wouldn't have had to drive along here at all.'

'Well, what do you want me to do? Push the car to the nearest village for you? Would that be sufficient penance?' She went and sat in the passenger seat, slamming the door behind her, her heart bumping with anger. After a time he joined her. He flipped open the glove compartment and pulled out an apple and a bar of chocolate.

'Supper,' he said, and proffered the apple. 'You eat half and I'll finish it.'

They ate in a hostile silence, which amplified their every bite and swallow. After a time she had an almost hysterical desire to laugh, but Luke's face told her that his thoughts were dark, and that no such levity was on his lips. After a time he spoke more quietly, although his voice was still cool and distant.

'Why don't you tell me about yourself, Bella Latham? Since we've got a whole night to fill.'

'You don't really want to know.'

He shrugged, looking ahead. 'It's conversation.'

'There's nothing much to tell. I'm not very interesting.'

'Let others be the judge of that. Where, for example did you grow up?'

'In Surrey. It was a perfectly normal upbringing. Then, when Mandy and I were eighteen, we both went to London. She studied at Guildhall and I went to London University and we took a flat together in West Kensington. . .'

Gradually the words began to come more easily, as he quizzed her expertly about the various stages of her life, until she even found herself confessing the terrible loneliness that had smitten her when Mandy had gone away to act in York and other towns around Britain.

'She was always the livelier one of the two of us, always the extrovert. And she was so worldly, while I was the one with her head buried in books all day. She solved all my problems for me, saw off any unwelcome admirers. When she left I felt as if I'd had a limb amputated.'

'So you replaced her as best you could?'

'How did you know?' Her eyes opened in surprise, meeting his directly for the first time since she had begun her saga.

He shrugged. 'It's obvious, it's what anyone would do.'

'I met a fellow student called Nick. We got engaged just three months after we met.'

'And?'

'It didn't work out. He——' she hesitated '——he ditched me. He said he was too young to settle down, and I was too clinging, too dependent. He was right, I know that now, although I didn't at the time.'

'So?'

'I learned to be independent, and throw myself into my own life. Now I wouldn't want it any other way.'

'You mean your career is your all?' She felt rather than saw his eyebrows arching sceptically.

'It means an awful lot to me.' There was an aggressive, defensive tone in her voice. 'There's so much work waiting to be done, and I know I can contribute something useful. Look at what happened today, at the conference—people were really interested in our findings.'

'It was an impressive performance,' he acknowledged.

'It was the high point of my career so far!' she cried, suddenly bitter again at the happenings of the day, 'And you spoilt it!'

His eyes bored into her, dark as thunder. 'I could say the same,' he grated. 'Exactly the same. In the same tone of voice. But I don't want to get into that whole argument again. Not here, not now, when we've still got an awful lot of hours in which we have to endure each other's company. In fact, just to make sure we don't, I'm going to stretch my legs.' He slammed the door hard and his footsteps faded swiftly into the darkness, leaving her utterly alone.

Miserably she chewed her last square of chocolate, staring blankly out at nothing. The night was growing cold, and she shivered and drew her jacket more tightly round her, and after a time she realised she was straining to hear his footsteps again, because even a hostile and accusing Luke was better company than the confused desolation of her own thoughts.

But it must have been an hour or more before he returned, still grim-faced. 'Well, I've established there's no sign of life for several miles in either direction. We'd better make our bed and lie on it.'

She looked at him, startled. He laughed harshly. 'Don't worry. It's much too cold to contemplate a night of unrestrained passion. And anyway, I'm far too angry with you to dare to lay a finger on you.'

'I wouldn't dream of letting you, even if you wanted to,' she snapped. 'Good, then as least we're agreed on one thing, he gritted. 'Now help me get these back seats down and one of us, at least, can try and get a reasonable night's sleep.'

When the job was done he insisted that she should be the one to climb into the back and settle herself under the old car rug they had found bundled on the floor, while he hunched down as best he could in the passenger seat. She was not exactly comfortable, her suit felt awkward and stiff, but at least she could stretch her legs out, and after a time of lying tense and self-conscious, listening to Luke's breathing, she slipped into a surprisingly deep sleep.

Later, something woke her. She did not know what it was—it might have been the call of a night bird or a sound from within the car. Whatever it was, she was awake in a moment, remembering exactly where she was and why. She lifted herself on to an elbow and looked at Luke. In the ghostly light of the summer's night, his profile looked stern and carved like stone, and his eyes stared broodingly out of the window. With one finger he rubbed his lips, lost in his own thoughts. It was plain he was not sleeping, and had not slept.

'What are you thinking?' She hadn't realised she was going to speak.

He turned, looking at her tumbled hair and sleepy eyes.

'About the movie,' he said, after a pause. 'What else?'

'What time is it?'

'Three o'clock.'

'You can't be comfortable. We should swop.'

He shook his head. 'Go back to sleep, Bella. I'm OK.'

'You won't be, in the morning, if you haven't slept at all. And you'll have work to do when we get back.'

He frowned, pushing a hand through his hair. 'I can't have you sitting up here all night.'

'Then, look,' she moved over, 'there's plenty of room here. It's stupid to waste it.'

His eyes went to the empty space, then stripped back to hers. She saw a wariness in them that made her explode. 'Oh, for heaven's sake, I'm not propositioning you! I've not the slightest interest in doing such a thing! And anyway, as you said yourself, it's hardly the circumstances for heady passion. It just seems daft not to use the space there is, and you'll never get any sleep unless you can stretch out.'

He looked at her, not moving, and she flushed, angry with the embarrassment of rejection. 'Well, it's up to you whether you want to behave like an adult or an adolescent! *I'm* going back to sleep.' And she flung herself back down, on her side, facing away from him.

A moment or two later she heard him laugh a little, under his breath, then crawl over beside her. She held her breath, then let it out slowly, careful to stay separated from him by a vital inch or two, but even apart like that they gave each other a welcome warmth, and both slipped swiftly down into sleep.

Yet some time in the night they must have rolled together, their unconscious selves reaching out for each other in sleep. Because when she woke she found to her astonishment that she was cradled in Luke's arms, her head pillowed gently against his shoulder, his hand holding her shoulder close.

It was the warm smell of his skin in her nostrils that first alerted her to the change, then her eyes fluttered open to see his white shirt and dark suit next to her eyes. She closed her eyes quickly, not wanting to wake and find the moment gone, and luxuriated shamelessly in the strength of his arms around her and the heedless tangle of their legs.

Then her eyes opened again to find his face. He was deeply asleep still, his lashes lowered, his lips closed. But even as she looked he stirred and his fingers tightened on her shoulder.

'It seems our bodies know something we don't.' His low murmur hardly moved his lips.

Her eyes went over him, and she saw a wicked glint of his eyes through half-open lids, and began to pull away.

'No.' He stopped her. 'Stay there, Bella. I want to look at you.'

She looked at him while his eyes slowly roamed her face, taking in her every feature. The car windows were misted up against the grey light of dawn, and there was no sound outside. They could have been anywhere in the world, or nowhere.

'So beautiful,' he murmured, and she saw him swallow, while her lips softened and parted, ready for his kisses. But, instead of gathering her to him, he shifted himself away from her, releasing her and turning on to his back, sighing deeply.

'And now,' he said slowly, 'for the problems of the day.'

CHAPTER TWELVE

LUKE was clever, though, Bella thought later in the day. Clever enough to know that he would never get the performance from her that he needed to finish his film unless he charmed away her angry aggression. That was why he had cradled her so warmly this morning, and why he remained considerate and thoughtful towards her throughout the long, frustrating hours that followed. And it worked, she thought bitterly. How it worked! Because now, when he looked at her, her blood fizzed along her veins, and when he smiled or brushed against her in passing her heart knocked against her ribs like a prisoner trying to get out. She was in thrall to him, her anger muted, and utterly helpless to still her body's clamouring desires.

There was a lot of time to think, that day. No vehicle passed them until well after breakfast-time, and then the van driver who picked them up insisted on finishing his delivery round to the local farms before driving them on to the nearest garage. And even after that there were further problems. The elderly, unhurried mechanic tut-tutted for a long time over the state of the wheel before pronouncing that there was nothing he could do, and that a new one would have to be delivered from town.

'But how long will that take?'

'Oh, they may be able to get one up here by teatime, if you're lucky.'

'Teatime! I can't wait until then!' Luke's frustration had been building all morning. Now he stepped forward as if he would take the man by his collar and

143

shake some sense of urgency into him. She saw his face harden.

'Luke!' She stepped forward quickly. 'Couldn't you hire a car or something, and go on ahead? I'll wait for the wheel and drive on later.'

His brain turned rapidly. 'Would you be OK on your own?'

'Yes, of course. As long as you leave me directions.'

His eyes snapped to the mechanic. 'Could you do that? Hire me a car?'

'Nope. But John Lewis, down the hill, could.'

'Take me there, then, pronto. You can put it all on the bill. And look after this young lady, will you? She hasn't eaten since yesterday lunchtime, and she'd probably like a wash, too.'

Impatient type, isn't he, your gentleman friend?' said the mechanic, coming back later.

'His time's precious at the moment. He's a film director, and everything comes to a halt if he's not there.' She wondered why she was bothering to defend him, and why she hadn't contradicted the man's assumption about their relationship.

'Oh, ah, heard about that film lot up the top of the valley. Even so, he drove off as if the hounds of hell were after him.'

She smiled. 'He likes to be in control. Unexpected punctures aren't part of his plan.'

'They aren't part of anyone's plan,' said the man comfortably, 'but we all have to learn to live with them. Now let's see what my wife can find you to eat.'

Darkness had settled over the hills again by the time the wheel had been delivered and fitted, and Bella was able to set off thankfully towards the film location.

She grinned grimly at the thought that yesterday it was the last place on earth she had wanted to go to, but tonight she could hardly wait to arrive where there was warmth, heat, food, hot water—and Luke.

Irritated, she shook her head, wishing she could free it of thoughts of him, but no matter how she tried she still saw his every gesture in her mind's eye, every expression of his compelling grey eyes, and only by concentrating hard on the road ahead could she manage to clear her brain. But after a time, as the road wound more steeply up into the mountains, she had no option but to frown at the narrow track ahead and pray she had not taken a wrong turning.

At last she found the white gate she had been looking for, and the pot-holed track up to a grey-stone farmhouse.

'You finally made it.' Luke materialised out of the night almost before the noise of the engine had died into the thick darkness. He opened her door and helped her out.

'Ow. I'm stiff,' she said, stumbling against his shoulder on the uneven ground. She quickly straightened away from him, burning from the contact. 'Do you know the wheel didn't arrive till nearly six, and then they all sat round having a cup of tea before getting themselves together to go and fit it?'

'I can believe it. I would have blown a gasket if I'd had to stay and chew my fingernails all afternoon. As it was, I got back in time to call a script conference. You can imagine how grateful I felt for your offer.'

She felt his eyes looking down warmly at her and glowed inside.

The furniture at Edwards farm was sparsely functional; the curtains and carpets clashed. 'It's normally a holiday cottage,' he said, as he led the way indoors, 'and, since most of us are out all day, it didn't seem worth making a fuss about the furnishings. Anyway, it's better upstairs.'

'How many people are staying here?'

'Only four. Most of them have gone off to the distant pub.'

'But where's everyone else living?'

'Spread out all over the place. Quite a lot are staying in the pub, that's about five miles away, and then we've taken over every free cottage we could get our hands on in the area. Mandy had a room here—for the extremely short duration of her stay—but we can sort something else out for you tomorrow, if you'd rather.'

Her heart sank deeply at the mention of Mandy, the memory of exactly why she was here.

'I've been thinking that I ought to know more about just what happened with Mandy,' she said despondently, 'before I face Guy and everyone else.' She raised tired eyes to meet his look and saw his lips curve as he saw the strain in her face.

'Later. Let's sort you out first. Why don't you have a bath, and I'll find you something to eat?'

'A bath would be blissful,' she said with feeling, only too willing to put off any uncomfortable conversations until later.

'Then come on up and I'll show you around.'

He put her briefcase on a bed and showed her the bathroom. From somewhere—she did not enquire where—he rustled up a hairdrier, some toiletries and a bath robe before departing downstairs announcing supper would be in half an hour. But once she slipped into the hot water she wanted to stay there forever, soaking away her tiredness, and it was nearly an hour before she got herself out and finished drying her hair. A knock at the bedroom door made her jump.

'Come in.'

'I'm expiring from starvation. I've brought up your pre-dinner drink to hurry you along.'

She ignored the glass of red wine he set on the desk.

'This is *your* room,' she said accusingly, waving the hairdrier around at the double bed piled with papers and scripts, the open suitcase on the floor. The wide arms of the navy silk bathrobe flapped about her. She guessed that was his, too.

'You can sleep here tonight. I'll doss down somewhere. There are no longer any sheets on Mandy's bed, and heaven knows where we'd find them. I'll ask Caroline in the morning. She's staying here, too.'

'What a surprise!'

His eyes narrowed. 'And just what is that supposed to mean?'

'Only what I said.'

'Where else would you expect my assistant to stay? Ten miles across the valley?'

'No, I'd expect your *assistant*,' she emphasised the word cruelly, 'to stay right here by your side.'

He stepped round very slowly so he could see her face, and a cruel grin crooked his mouth.

'Why, I do believe you're jealous.'

Bella set the hairdrier down on the dresser with a crack. 'Don't be absurd. Why should I be jealous?'

'It's an interesting question. And one I don't know the answer to.'

'I'll tell you the answer. I'm not jealous! I've no reason to be jealous! I don't give a damn whether Caroline is your lover, mistress, assistant or long-lost sister! All I am is tired, angry and fed up to the nines with this whole stupid business!'

Her spurting, confused anger kindled an instant

response in him. The grin left his face as if wiped off by an unseen hand. 'Do you think you're the only one? When I found out what you and Mandy had been up to, I was so furious you're lucky I didn't come straight up to London and drag you back here by the hair!'

'You mean I'm lucky you barged in on the biggest conference in my field this year, and showed me up in front of three hundred people!'

'Consider yourself fortunate I didn't up-end you in front of all your colleagues and give you a damned good hiding!'

'I've considered you a lot of things, Luke Retford, but I didn't know you got your kicks that way!' Her voice snapped with hysterical sarcasm.

'Why, you little——!' He stepped forward and gripped her wrist sharply, a tic of anger at his jaw. For a second she was frightened of him. Then she saw his own tiredness and tension, the black marks of exhaustion beneath his eyes, and shame tempered her anger. 'I'm sorry,' she got out tightly. 'That was a cheap jibe.' She pulled her wrist away and rubbed it, staring at him with wide eyes. 'How did you find out anyway? About Mandy and me?'

His eyes lingered on her, grey with conflicting emotions, then he walked away and picked up his glass of wine, draining it in one swallow.

'I told you. Mandy might look like you at first glance, but she puts out quite different vibrations.' He looked up, hard and rawly at her. 'She did nothing for me at all, left me quite cold. Whereas you and I only have to be within a hundred yards of each other to set the very air jumping.'

She swallowed, breathless, watching him.

'It's true, isn't it, Bella?' he insisted. 'It was true in Mauritius, and it's still true here.'

She hesitated. 'Yes.'

There was a long, thick silence. What now? she wondered. What will he do now? Tension surrounded them like dense fog. She shut her eyes, feeling faint at the admission she had just made. Surely he would come to her now, touch her, hold her? He had to, he just had to. But his voice broke the silence, snapping the unbearable tension.

'There wasn't any great scene, if that's what you're worrying about. I spent the first morning scarcely believing the evidence of my eyes. There was Mandy, completely the same yet utterly different. I wondered if it was me—if all that tropical moonlight had coloured my judgement and warped my memories. No one else seemed to notice anything wrong.' He looked at her with a hard look and his voice was cold. She shivered at his tone. 'I let her do the first take, and then I knew for sure it was not just me—the chemistry was completely different. Poor old Guy was left shaking his head and wondering if he'd been hitting the bottle too hard again, while Mandy herself was shaking with nerves and kept glancing at me as if I were about to put her before a firing squad.

'Then I went over to her, to show her how I wanted her to angle her head for a particular shot. Like this.' He came across the room to her and held her head, his fingers splaying across the angles of her jaw, and the touch of his fingers made her shudder with desire. 'And I knew at once that she really *was* a different person.'

'How?'

His voice hoarsened. 'Because of this.' With a forefinger he traced the thin seam of bramble scar at her neck. 'It wasn't there.'

'You noticed that? It's so tiny!' She was shaking

under his hands.

'I doubt if there's a single thing about you I haven't noticed,' he said thickly. Then his hands pulled her head up to his and his lips punished her with a hard, angry, impatient kiss.

'Oh!' He took all the breath from her lungs. His body backed her to the wall as he moved to hold her tightly, furiously, his lips not leaving hers but opening her mouth with an unleashed need that made her head spin. He was dominating her, crushing her to him, and she should have protested, but she could not, because she felt exactly the same anger, the same desperate need, and she shook in his arms with the force of her feelings.

He was breathing hard when he broke his mouth from hers, and his eyes were burning. 'It all fell into place in an instant. I knew even before I quizzed her what had happened, the whole story, right from the beginning, although at the same time I could hardly believe that anyone in their right mind would pull such a crazy stunt.'

'But how could you? We were so careful!'

He released her and put up his hand to tick off his fingers. 'That time you came to see me in my office—that awful, amateurish flirting! It made me feel right away there was something about you that didn't ring true. In fact I seriously considered dropping Mandy Latham from the picture altogether after that interview. Then I bumped into you the next day, didn't I, outside my office? You looked pretty different in your pony-tail and your jeans, but I knew. Somewhere deep in my subconscious, I knew. Although why in heaven you came back to the scene of your crime I've no idea.'

She flushed under his scrutiny, but heard herself

saying, 'Go on.' Her fascination with his thought processes was stronger than her embarrassment.

'Your whole demeanour in Mauritius—your nervous panic, and the way you didn't seem to know, or want to know, the first thing about filming. I was too busy to dwell on it much at the time, but it niggled away at the back of my mind. Then what finally clinched it was seeing your room, all those books and files you forget to hide—and your feeble explanation when I asked you about them.'

She suddenly felt very small and naïve, and turned away from him to rest her heated forehead on the whitewashed wall behind her. But his voice ripped on relentlessly, 'Even so, the puzzle didn't make any pattern until Mandy turned up here. After her first take, I asked Caroline to phone her agent for some biographical details, and that's where we found out about the twin sister. After that it was the easiest thing in the world to put two and two together and make four. The only missing part was why? But when I confronted Mandy, and told her in no uncertain terms that I knew what she'd been up to, she immediately confessed the whole sorry story.'

'I suppose you gave her a hard time?'

'What do you think? I've got the best part of a million pounds and a year of my life tied up in this project. Not to mention the concerted efforts of several hundred other people.'

'Poor Mandy.'

'Poor Mandy indeed. She couldn't wait to get the first train out. Although, when I'd calmed down enough to think about it more clearly, I hardly knew whether to laugh or cry. It seemed such a pathetic little duplicity.'

She whirled round. 'I don't see what's so pathetic

about wanting to help someone who's desperate! If you'd seen her face when she realised! I *had* to do something for her. I couldn't just let her suffer.'

'Mandy's only one person among many,' he bit back. 'You might have paused to think about the repercussions on everyone else of your little prank.'

'Oh, why won't you understand? It wasn't a prank. We didn't do it for fun! It wasn't any fun at all for me, being in Mauritius! It was one of the most miserable weeks of my life.'

'Oh, really?' He stepped closer, putting his hands against the wall on either side of her head so she was forced to stare ahead at him. She had never felt so acutely aware of his strength and his power. 'I rather got the impression you enjoyed at least one or two moments of your stay.'

She tossed her hair, more bravely than she felt. 'And what's that meant to mean?'

'You know full well, Bella,' he said dangerously. 'It's what we agreed on earlier—what we do to each other——'

'Don't——' But he was holding her shoulders, searching her eyes, powerful in his anger and desire.

'I've thought about you constantly since Mauritius, day and night,' he rapped out. 'Every time I shut my eyes I see a vision of you walking naked out of the sea. You'll never know what it cost me to turn and walk away from you that night. Then later, when we were together in your room—I tell you, Bella, I didn't know what was happening to me. I've been around beautiful actresses all my working life, but most of them left me fairly indifferent. Then along comes this one, wrapped in mystery, and I'm hooked. And even when I find out what the mystery is all about, when I discover I'm the poor fool who's been duped—I still find I'm as

devastated by her as ever. Sometimes I feel I hate you
for that, for what you've done to me——'

His words choked on the rasp of his throat and in
their place his lips descended swiftly to her neck,
catching her flesh with an urgent, biting kiss that sent
a hot shaft of sensation arrowing through her. His lips
dragged hotly against her skin, torrid with desire, and
his fingers gripped her shoulders hard.

'I want you,' he said tightly, 'How I want you!' and
his hands moved up to cup and mould the fullness of
her breasts.

The savagery of his unmasked need inflamed her
beyond even the thought of resistance. She groaned
his name as he lifted her to the bed and sank his head
to her breasts, taking their aching tips with his lips
through the thin silk that he had not the patience to
push aside.

'Oh!' Her body was alight, aching, drumming its
needs, as he found her mouth again and devoured it
with hard kisses, and his hands loosened her robe so
that he could know the length of her beneath him.

She felt every bone and muscle of him against her,
and his arousal, his pent-up energy, made her gasp
and tear at his shirt to bring his naked flesh against
hers.

'Here.' He pulled away from her and swiftly
stripped her of her robe, and himself of his clothes,
then gathered her to him again, covering her fiercely
with his body.

He was perfect, she thought, as her hands roamed
his shoulders and his hips, perfect in every part, and
she trembled in his arms at their sudden, headlong
lovemaking.

Somewhere, in the distant whirling part of her mind,
she felt doubts stir, but her need to be close to him, to

yield to him and to hold him to her, obliterated them with urgent desire. And it felt right, so right, to be together like this, holding each other length to length, while he kissed her and groaned his need. And it seemed to her heightened senses that she was as close to his thoughts as she was to his body, so that she knew as he struggled to check himself that his raging desire, so long penned back, would not be tamed.

So it was she who moved beneath him, breathing her assent, and when he moved inside her his thrusting need pushed them both towards a swift and violent explosion of passion.

Slowly his breathing steadied again. He raised himself on one elbow to look at her and gently touched her face. 'You understood,' he said, and his eyes were wondering.

The sight of him made her throat ache with the intensity of the feelings inside her, his broad shoulders and strong chest, his tousled hair and even mouth and his eyes still glowing like grey coals, and she gloried in the feeling of his warm flesh against hers. He sank his head against her collar and rested, and in the silence her head reeled from the suddenness and the shock of all that had just happened between them.

But as her blood beat more evenly again, and the chill of the mountain night crept over her flesh, the doubts crept back. What was she thinking of? This man beside her, his arm flung across her body, was a stranger. He did not care for her in the least. All he felt for her was a raging desire—or maybe something even less: a desirous rage. Certainly there had been an anger in his lovemaking that had taken her to dizzy heights, but now dropped her down into a pit of loneliness and regret.

'Luke?' Her voice was tremulous.

She waited a long time, but his even breathing told her the worst. He had taken his fill of her and now he had turned away into exhausted sleep. Near tears, she curled on her side and waited miserably for morning to come.

CHAPTER THIRTEEN

SOMETHING woke Bella in the thin light of early morning. She swam languorously up from the depths of sleep, stretching and murmuring like a cat, her misery of the night only a distant memory, for her dreams had been surprisingly sweet and she felt strangely safe and loved in Luke's arms.

Now his fingers were moving sensually on her breast, touching her with a gentle possession. It was this that had woken her, this achingly sweet caress that stiffened her body against his hand and made him gather her closer against him.

He kissed her neck, and spoke softly in her ear. 'Turn round,' he commanded, 'I want to look at you.'

She moved to him, her eyelids opening slowly, and he looked for a long time into her face with a dark and complex look that she could not fathom.

She did not even want to, she thought hazily, putting her arms out to him. All she wanted was for this warm sweetness to last forever.

'Bella,' he murmured, 'I thought this would never happen.'

Her heart squeezed within her as she raised her face to feel his lips again, and he took her mouth with an agonising gentleness.

'I was so angry last night,' he admitted, against her mouth. 'Angry because of what you'd done to me, and angry because you made me need you so badly.' He kissed her again, long and yearningly, his tongue tasting the sweetness of her mouth, and the kiss seemed to reach down into every atom of her

156

being. 'Not now, though, not any more. Now I really want to make love to you.'

He shifted in the bed and reached for her arms, spreading them on the bed and pinning her wrists lightly with his hands so she was in his power. Then he kissed her again, her lips, her eyes, her jaw, her throat, conjuring gasps from her lips at the feelings he aroused.

She was helpless as his lips moved lower, taking her breasts, then the soft skin of her stomach, but she felt no fear of him, only a deeply welling pleasure. Slowly he began to learn every inch of her body, touching her wonderingly and telling her his pleasure. But he held himself from her, intent only on rousing her beyond thought, until her aching arms could bear it no longer and she reached out to pull him down against her.

Her hands roamed his back, learning the shape of his lean hips and muscled legs. She felt the patterning of dark hair graze against her breasts, and the way their legs tangled together, and she wondered if she could bear it a moment longer.

But then there was no thought of time, of anything, as Luke continued to touch her, kiss her, rouse her way beyond a point she had ever known before, so that when he finally moved inside her they were both cast adrift on a limitless ocean of sweet, sensual pleasure that finally drowned them both in shuddering fulfilment.

She held him close to her as their tide of pleasure slowly ebbed, feeling his back damp with sweat and hearing his ragged breath in her ear, and she thought with sudden piercing clarity, I love you. And for a second the thought was so strong that she could not be sure she had not spoken the words aloud.

Then Luke moved, raising himself to look at her. 'Bella.'

'What is it?' He sounded moved, she thought, almost shocked, and her hands tightened protectively.

He shook his head, then said with a smile that caught at her heart, 'I've always wondered what they meant when they talked about the earth moving. I think I've just found out.'

She searched his eyes. 'I know I have.' She smiled, looking at him, feasting her eyes on his beautiful body, loving him. Somehow, without their noticing it, it had got lighter and the birds were singing outside the window. She wanted to sing, too. She loved Luke, and he had just made love to her exquisitely, with true warmth and tenderness.

He leaned over to kiss her once more then lay back.

'I ought to have known that a woman who can't resist flinging herself naked into the tropical ocean would have such a passionate nature, only you disguise it very well.'

'What do you mean?'

'I mean you looked so prim and proper, standing up on the platform yesterday, in your businesswoman's suit, delivering your lecture—no one would believe you were the same woman!'

'Well, I am, I am.'

He turned his head on the pillow and looked at her.

'You do know that most of the men in that room were sitting there daydreaming about getting you into bed? I watched them all undressing you with their eyes.' He grinned. 'I wanted to punch them all on the nose!'

Her eyes lit. 'Now *you're* jealous!'

'Yes, I admit it.' His eyes darkened and he said rawly. 'I'm jealous of all your previous lovers, Bella.'

Her heart lurched at his tone. 'There's only been one. There hasn't been anyone since Nick.'

'No one?'

'No one at all. Oh, there very nearly was——' He propped himself on his elbow and scowled down into her eyes. 'In Mauritius. Only he left me and he didn't come back.'

He smiled, and then the smile faded as he heard and understood the hurt behind her words.

'Did you really want me to? I wanted to, but I was sure you would have locked the door on me. I felt I was seducing you into something you didn't want.'

'And now?' She gestured at the bed.

He held her eyes then bent to kiss her again. 'I think that nothing in this universe could have stopped me making love to you last night, Bella Latham. I'd waited too long, and endured too much. But I don't feel the slightest bit guilty. Now I know it's something we both want,' he paused to kiss her, 'something we both want very much indeed.'

She was absurdly happy, even though Luke left her before breakfast, his mind already busy with the problems of the day. She drifted back into sleep and woke late, and found herself humming as she bathed and made coffee and waited for the car which would drive her to the village, to buy essentials for her stay, and then on into the hills to where the shooting was taking place.

Her happiness seemed infectious. When she breezed into the wardrobe department to ask for some jeans and T-shirts, hastily inventing a lie about a lost suitcase, the girls there just tut-tutted in sympathy. Neither they nor anyone else seemed to know that she was Bella, not Mandy. And Guy, who did, simply gave her a warm hug and said she didn't have to explain anything. 'I guess Luke's already said his piece. And, anyway, it's just nice to have you back on board.'

Her acting, too, seemed blessed with a surprising new confidence. She was in touch with her body and her feelings, in a way she had never known before, and it showed in her every move and gesture. She knew instinctively what Luke wanted from her, and when their eyes met in private understanding she thrilled deep inside at her new and intimate knowledge of him. All day she floated on air, impatient for night to fall so she could be in his arms again.

They filmed late, under lights, and ate supper on the set, so when she finally got back to the farmhouse she went straight upstairs to soak in the bath and to wait for Luke to finish working and drive back to her. Revived, she stepped out of the hot water and took his robe from the hook on the back of the door and, wrapping it round her, walked into his room.

'Who's that?'

'What the——?' She jumped at the sound.

'You!' Caroline was looking up, startled at the intrusion, from the desk where she sat. Behind her was an open door, leading to her adjoining bedroom.

The scene, with all its implications, etched itself indelibly into Bella's mind in that one split second. She was dumbstruck, frozen. How could she ever have forgotten about Caroline? But she had, completely and utterly.

'What are you doing in here?' Caroline's voice was furious.

Bella tipped her chin defiantly. If there was to be a fight, at least she was on the winning side. 'What do you think I'm doing?'

Caroline's cold eyes ripped over her tousled hair, Luke's robe.

'This is Luke's room. Your room is downstairs. Someone should have shown you to it when you arrived.'

Bella stared straight back at her with a deep violet gaze. 'I arrived last night.'

Caroline stood up, knocking her chair over. 'What do you mean?'

'What do you think I mean?'

Anger suffused Caroline's features. 'Haven't you caused enough trouble, Mandy? Or should I say Bella? Don't you know Luke despises you for what you've done? Your cheap little trick?'

'Really? He has a funny way of showing it. If that's his anger, I wouldn't mind seeing more of it.' She felt invincible, still wrapped around with happiness. Caroline was out of the game. She had no power to hurt her.

But Caroline was gathering her defenses, laughing with forced scorn. 'Just because Luke has slept with you doesn't mean a thing. He's wanted to get you into bed since Mauritius. No doubt finding out how you'd tricked him only made him more determined. But now he's made his conquest he'll lose all interest, you mark my words. I've seen it all before!'

'Well, we'll just wait and see, shall we?'

Caroline turned away, feigning indifference. 'Of course, last night was ideal,' she said casually. 'He knew I was away in London for a couple of days. I wonder how he plans to deal with the situation from now on.'

'I'm sure he'll find a way. I'll simply wait and see.' Bella knew he would come. What had happened between them was too powerful to ignore, and she was surer than she had ever been of anything that he wanted her with the same passion as she wanted him.

'You'll have a long wait,' Caroline said nastily. 'He's had to drive down to Cardiff this evening. I doubt if he'll be back.'

'Don't be ridiculous. I've just seen him on the set, not an hour ago.'

'Oh, yes? And did you see one of the lighting crew fall off the scaffolding? Luke's taken him off to be X-rayed. He's just sent me a message.'

'You're joking?' But Bella could see in Caroline's eyes that she wasn't. Her protective shell of happiness began to crack apart. How could he have told Caroline and not her? The answer was all too horribly clear. Caroline must be right. She was a ship that passed in the night—in her case, last night—whereas Caroline was a permanent fixture.

'No.' Caroline held up a piece of paper from her pocket.

Bella took it and read it slowly. 'I'm sorry, darling, I won't be back tonight. Fred Johnson seems to have fractured his wrist and needs speeding down to casualty in Cardiff. I doubt if we'll be back tonight. Cruel fate, eh? All this time apart and then this happens. I miss you. Luke.' And the bottom of the paper had some hastily scrawled kisses.

Bella sank down slowly on the bed and Caroline plucked the paper from her fingers and pocketed it again. 'Oh, and if you want something to while away the long, lonely evening you might be interested in this.' She offered Bella a weighty document in place of the flimsy scrap of paper.

'What is it?'

'The revised script. They've changed the ending yet

again.'

Woodenly Bella held out her hand for the script.

'By the time Grayson catches up with Dee, she's embroiled in a passionate affair with a new boyfriend—she's satisfied in every way,' Caroline said sarcastically. 'It might give you another clue about why Luke was in such a hurry to get you between the sheets. Since you're no natural actress, he knows it's up to him to get you into the right frame of mind for the final scenes. It would never have suited his purposes to have you uptight with frustration, would it?'

'Luke wouldn't do that!'

'Luke would walk barefoot through a pit of poisonous snakes if he thought it would mean a better movie.' Caroline's mouth twisted harshly. 'You don't know the first thing about him, do you? Oh, he's a fine enough stud all right, but that's probably about the only time in his life that he actually thinks about anything but his work. And when the action's over, then it's straight back to the movies! Take it from one who knows. Why, I bet he'd forgotten you by the time he began to do his shirt buttons up this morning.'

'Oh!' Bella blinked away a painful memory of Luke's absorbed face as he had dressed that morning. 'You're only saying that because it's how you want it to be,' she managed to counter, but her heart had gone out of the fight. And anyway, Caroline was already turning and whisking out of the door.

Bella spent a long, wakeful night in the narrow bed that had been Mandy's, her skin irritated by the sheetless blankets and her thoughts raw with humiliation and loss. But she could not forget the words of Luke's note, and she gradually came to know that Caroline must be right. The new script cried out for a girl so sure and certain of her new love that nothing could touch her invincible happiness. It was how she had felt all yesterday, exactly how she had acted the part, and Luke must have been well satisfied with the way he had manipulated her.

For Grayson, though, it was not a happy ending, she noted. His scenes with Dee were raw and painful, and when he was finally forced to leave it was with empty hands and a heavy heart. When he drove back to London, in the final shot, it was as a man thinking bitterly about his own lonely future, independent of the girl he had come to love.

She bit her lips grimly. No doubt she would be thinking the same bitter thoughts when she headed back for London, but a future without Luke anywhere in it seemed unutterably bleak and empty.

At the set the next day, Luke was already busy, ordering about cameras and lights, but he broke away at once when he saw her arrive.

'Bella,' he said quickly, reaching for her elbows.

She tore her arms down. 'Don't you dare touch me!'

'What?'

She glared at him, so wretched and furious she could not speak. He was so handsome, so powerful—so utterly ruthless.

'What is it?' he repeated, impatience creeping into his shocked tone.

'You——' She choked. 'Last night.'

He frowned. 'I had to take Fred to hospital. Surely you understand? The poor guy's got a broken wrist. And I had to wait to drive him back here.'

'Oh, I understand! I understand everything! All too clearly. I wish I didn't!'

He cursed, angry and perplexed. 'There isn't time

now. We'll have to sort this out later.'

'There isn't any sorting out to be done. As far as I'm concerned, it's all over. Finished.'

'What is?'

'Us. Whatever there was to it—which wasn't much!'

There was a figure at his elbow. 'Luke, we need to get rolling if we're going to catch this sunshine.' He turned at the interruption, cursing again, then back to Bella.

'I don't understand what's got into you!' he hissed.

'Some sense! That's what's got into me! Sense enough to see what you were up to!' Her eyes blazed up to his. 'I'll stay here and I'll finish your film for you, Luke Retford! I'll do it for Mandy's sake. That's the only reason! But when it's over I'll be on the fastest train out of here, and I hope I never see you in my life again!'

He glared at her darkly, a pulse ticking in his jaw, his thoughts turning furiously, then he turned on his heel and clapped his hands loudly. 'OK, everyone, to work—and make it good.'

Somehow Bella got through the day. It almost helped to feel so hollow and angry. When Dee spat angry, rejecting words at Grayson, she put all the venom of her feelings towards Luke into them, and the scene was so good it drew spontaneous applause from the crew when it ended.

She ignored it, and set straight off down the narrow track towards the farmhouse. It was a walk of several miles, but she felt she had enough furious energy to stride halfway back to London.

'Bella, wait. I want an explanation!' Luke came after her. He caught at her elbow, but she marched on, snatching it away. 'Why, you—!' This time he caught her hard, his fingers biting into her flesh. 'What are you playing at this time?'

'I'm not playing at anything. I'm going back to my room.'

'I want to know what's happened to you.'

She turned to him, blazing. 'I'll tell you what's happened! I was foolish enough to let myself go in for a one-night stand! It's never happened before and it won't happen again! Now let me go.'

'One night? Who says it has to be one night?'

'I gather that's what you're famous for!'

'You gather wrong! You should check your facts!'

'My source is impeccable.'

'And what's that meant to mean?'

'I mean it's from someone who knows you rather better than I do!' She looked round desperately at the wild purple hills all around. But they were blurred and fogged with her tears.

She saw him hesitate, his thoughts churning. 'Tell me.' It was a rapped command.

'Work it out for yourself. You're an intelligent man, aren't you?'

Abruptly she tore herself free and began to hurry and stumble away. He ran after her. She heard his boots slithering on the loose scree, then he was blocking her path.

'Rumour and gossip are rife on film sets, I've told you that before. I don't know who's been whispering what malice in your ear, but I would have expected you to be able to rise above it all.'

'As you do, you mean? You just take what you want and ignore everyone else!'

'Me? I thought it was what *we* wanted. I hardly felt I was forcing myself on you that night!'

'It was,' she cried. 'You're right, it was. It was what

I wanted! I've never felt like that about any man before: I still do,' she confessed wildly. 'I've only got to look at you to want to touch you, hold you——'

He grasped her shoulders, shaking her in his anger, 'Then why in heaven's——?'

'Because you're just—it's just——' The words were choking in her throat. In front of her eyes his chest heaved. She could see the column of his throat, feel his hands on her shoulder. 'I——' She looked up to find words, but his lips came down on hers, hard and furious, and his hands pulled the curves of her hips hard against him. They flared together into instant wanting. She could feel his body harden immediately, as her own blood drummed in response.

'See what you do to me!' he cried.

'No!' She struggled in his arms, summoning every last inch of will-power. 'No!' She tore her head aside, sobbing, 'It's not right—not enough——'

'Then tell me what it is that you want, Bella,' he said cruelly.

She raised her head again, face tear-stained, lips trembling. That was simple. She wanted him to want her for herself alone. She wanted what she could never have, his honesty and his love.

'It's too late for what I want,' she said bitterly. 'It always was, right from the beginning. I was an utter fool to ever think differently.' With a toss of her head she stepped back from him and managed to meet his eyes levelly. 'Yes, I want you,' she cried bluntly. 'You want me. But that's no basis for a relationship—especially when I know you're busy twisting everything round for your own ends! I'm not a puppet, not a doll in your doll's house, and I'm not going to be manipulated by you any more!'

He exploded in exasperation. 'What the hell are you

talking about? Manipulation? I've never felt less in control of things in my life!'

'Oh, really? Well, all the evidence is against that.'

'I don't know what you're talking about.'

Her eyes blazed. 'Then why not ask your trusty assistant? Ask Caroline—she seems to understand things better than we do ourselves!' And she pushed past him and strode away down the valley.

CHAPTER FOURTEEN

LUKE came nowhere near Bella during her last days on the set, and when they worked together his attitude was crisply professional. It tore her apart to see his cold eyes, and hear his curt commands, but she steeled herself to remain cool and detached.

Once, she heard him come back, late, to the farmhouse, and it seemed as if he paused outside her door for several long minutes. Every muscle in her body was rigid, she was sure he would knock, but then his footsteps went slowly on by. The next day she even wondered if she had dreamed that hesitation outside her room, but when she arrived on the set she found it buzzing with the news that Luke Retford had actually allowed himself to get drunk last night—an unheard of thing—and was like a bear with a sore head this morning.

She watched miserably as Caroline hurried forward with water and aspirin for him, and she longed to get away back to London.

'I've never known him like this.' They were the first words Caroline had spoken to her since their row in his room.

'Well, you can't blame me this time,' she said tartly. 'I haven't been near him for days.' But Caroline knew that, she thought wretchedly—they must share his bed upstairs, while she lay alone in her tiny single room below.

'You'll live to learn that's not such a bad thing.' A bitter harshness in Caroline's voice made her look up. Caroline was watching Luke closely, but Bella noticed he never threw her as much as a glance.

'You mean he likes his women seen but not heard?' she said sarcastically.

'I don't know what he likes,' Caroline snapped. 'I only know he's not in the marriage market. Never has been, never will be. Although I must hand it to you—you're smarter than most. Some hang around him for months before they realise there's no hope.'

'Maybe I'm not in the marriage market either,' Bella flared, adding nastily, 'I'm surprised you don't see them all off sooner, a little guard dog like yourself. It must get quite exhausting, protecting your boss's interests as carefully as you do—I certainly hope he pays you well for all the many services you render.' Caroline flushed darkly and stalked away, leaving Bella to face the day more cast down than ever by her own unpleasantness.

But the next day was her last, and she counted the hours until the taxi was due to arrive to take her to the station. She was packing her few sparse things, nothing more than her briefcase and a carrier bag of possessions she had acquired here, when Luke walked in. He did not bother to knock, and his sudden arrival caused her to jump with shock.

'Oh! I didn't hear you.'

'I've brought you this.' It was a single wild pink rose, plucked from the hedgerow. 'I thought one flower would be easier to throw in the bin than a whole bouquet.' There was no emotion in his face as he spoke, no softening of his harsh gaze on her.

'Oh!' It was beautiful. Bella looked at him with astonishment. She had never imagined he was the sort of man who would make such a gesture, and there was a lump in her throat.

'It's to say "thank you". Thank you for doing such

a good job with Dee's part—under difficult circumstances. No matter how bad that little personal scene was between us, I want you to know I appreciate what you've done for the film.' He pushed a hand through his hair.

Her heart sank to her boots. 'Little personal scene?' Nothing could have spelled out more clearly what he thought about the night they had spent together.

'I don't want it! I don't want anything from you!'

He scoured her face and opened his mouth as if to speak. Then he hesitated and set his lips again.

'I knew you wouldn't accept anything more,' he said, 'but something as small as this——' .

'Nothing!'

She snatched it from his hand and threw it to the floor.

There was a long, difficult silence as they both looked at the flower, then he spoke tensely. 'I didn't mean to hurt you, Bella, I want you to know that. I thought—hell, I don't know what I thought! Maybe I wasn't thinking at all. But it was just one of those things—sometimes they happen. And we were good together.'

'Yes, we were, weren't we? Good together.' Her voice twisted with pain at the blunt phrase. 'But it's over now. And I, for one, plan to forget it ever happened.' She could not bring herself to look into those unfathomable grey eyes.

'Have you got a lift to the station?'

'Yes.'

He looked at her briefcase and carrier bag, ready on the bed. 'Well, that's it, then.'

'Yes.' Bella looked up quickly, and caught a strange look of pain in his eyes as he pushed a hand through his hair yet again. She swallowed. 'Goodbye, Luke.'

'Goodbye, Bella.'

And that was it, except that after he had closed the door behind him she had bent down quickly and picked the rose and its fallen petals from the floor and wrapped them carefully in a tissue before putting them in her bag.

Bella went back to London, and slowly over the following weeks the rose she had nursed all the way home with her withered to a faded husk. Mandy slowly revived from the dreadful dressing down Luke had given her, and, as rumours spread through the film world of her scorching performance in Luke Retford's latest movie, an exhilarating number of tempting offers came her way.

Back at the Institute of Health Bella found life in full swing again as lecturers and students returned from the long summer vacation. Pete, her co-worker, returned, brown from the Californian sun and full of praise for her performance at the Bristol conference. 'Look at these letters,' he grinned, scanning their mail. 'They're from all over the place. You've really put us on the map, Bell!' He read on. 'Hey! There's an offer here for you to work in Stockholm for a year. You should take it.'

'No, I don't feel like it.' She didn't feel like anything very much, and she was beginning to have the most dreadful suspicions about why.

It was because she was tired, she told herself firmly, and because she had had no proper holiday this year. And, anyway, emotional stress and trauma were well known for upsetting normal bodily rhythms.

But at home, alone, at night, she tried to face the facts. After all, she could all too easily be carrying Luke's child. On that one heedless night they had spent together she had thought of nothing except the joy of being with him.

What would she do if she was pregnant? She had no idea, except to know with complete certainty that she would have the baby, love it and rear it as best she could. Sometimes she shut her eyes and imagined what Luke's baby would look like—it would have dark, haunting eyes and wayward hair and an impatient intelligence—but at other times her mind veered away from such thoughts, drifting away into hopelessness, yearning reveries about their brief time of happiness.

But one morning, as she bent to pick the mail up from the mat, she felt a dull, familiar ache in her stomach. She knew she should have been glad that her worries had proved unfounded, yet instead of relief she felt only a searing stab of disappointment. Now she had no Luke, and no part of him either.

She sat at the kitchen table, turning the letters sightlessly in her hands, and the strength of her feelings shocked her through and through.

She had changed over the past few months, she thought, changed utterly. Before this summer she had been happy in her work, content to throw herself into her career. But then she had become an actress, digging down into the huge well of her repressed senses and feelings, and Luke had stirred those feelings further, making her melt with love and longing until the thought of life without him, without even his child, was unbearably bleak and empty.

'Oh, damn you, Luke Retford! I wish I'd never set eyes on you.' She tore at the top envelope in frustration and a thick, cream invitation fell out. She stared at it in total disbelief. It was an invitation to the Royal première of Luke's film.

'How dare you?' she shouted furiously to the empty kitchen. 'How dare you do this to me?'

As if in answer, the phone suddenly shrilled.

'Yes?'

'It's Luke. Don't put the phone down on me.' He spoke even as she began to slam the receiver back in place.

'Why did you invite me to the première? Haven't I done enough for you already?'

'More than you can ever begin to guess at!' There was an unsettling intensity in his voice that made her catch her breath.

'Then why——?'

'You should never have got that invitation,' he said rapidly. 'The publicity people sent it out by mistake. I planned to invite you—in fact, I wanted you to come as my partner—but I intended to offer the invitation in person.'

'You must be crazy!'

'Why crazy?'

'Oh!' She flung her hand up violently. 'Take Caroline! She's good enough for everything else!'

'Look, Caroline——' he broke off abruptly, with a muttered curse. 'I can't talk to you like this. I'm coming over.' And the phone went dead.

He was at her door in less than fifteen minutes, parking his car carelessly at an angle to the kerb and taking the steps two at a time. She watched his lithe, impatient figure from the window and the glorious sight of him was like a knife turning between her ribs.

He took in her pale face at once. 'You look terrible. Are you ill?'

She stared at his familiar, handsome face and hated him for making her love him so much.

'I thought I was pregnant,' she said baldly. 'I've just

found out I'm not. It's hardly the best time of the month for looking radiant.'

'Pregnant?' She saw dates reeling rapidly through his mind. 'You mean us—you've been worrying here alone for six weeks! Oh, Bella——'

'Save your sympathy,' she said shortly. 'I'm not. And, even if I were, I'd only blame myself.' Rudely she turned and marched into the living-room. He followed her.

'Are you alone?'

'Mandy's away doing a screen test.'

'The Dean Singer movie?'

She nodded , her eyes lifting to his face. She wanted to hate it, but she ached with bitter love for every familiar plane of it. 'Good,' he said. 'I put him on to her.'

Her eyes opened in surprise.

'Oh, yes.' His voice twisted. 'I'm not quite as selfish and self-centred as you want to think I am. It might surprise you to know that I felt pretty bad about Mandy, one way and another, and I've been doing my best to open a few doors for her.'

'I'm sure she'd like to thank you herself,' she snapped. 'As for me, it's nothing to me what you are.'

He looked at her, and suddenly all his normal self-possession seemed to desert him at the sight of her tense look and hating words.

'Do you mean that? Because if you do—if you really do—then I'll walk out of here this minute and never bother you again!'

'I——' His eyes burned on her like black fire. 'I——' To her horror, tears started to choke her throat. 'I don't know *what* I feel about you!' It was a lie. She loved him, she loved him completely, every infuriating inch of him.

He pushed a hand through his hair. It was a gesture she knew so well, the thing he always did when he was puzzled, or angry, or lost for words, and it sent a stab of anguish through her heart. He raised his hands, as if he longed to reach out for her, then dropped them to his side.

'Tell me what happened in Wales,' he said abruptly, 'to make you turn against me so suddenly.'

'Don't you know?'

'I can hazard a pretty good guess, but I'd prefer to hear it from the horse's mouth.'

She swallowed. 'You didn't come back that night——' she started, but he cut in at once.

'No—and I sent a message over to explain why. I asked for it to be left in my room, where I knew you'd see it.'

Her eyes flew to his. 'There was a note! Caroline said it was for her.'

'Caroline,' he said flatly. 'She probably hoped it was for her. You thought she was my lover, didn't you? You put two and two together and made five.'

'She as good as told me so.'

'Did she?'

She shivered at the tense anger behind his words. 'Are you saying she isn't?'

'She isn't.'

'What——?' She felt her world breaking apart, but the broken pieces made no new pattern. 'You mean there's nothing between you?'

'Nothing now. Nothing for years. We had a brief affair years ago, when she first came to work for me. It was over in weeks—at least, it was for me. But Caroline has always hoped we could revive it.'

'And you let her carry on working for you!'

He had the grace to flush a little. 'I'm not perfect,

Bella. She's a first-class assistant, and her devotion has, on the whole, been more of a help than a hindrance. She wanted to stay, and I let her, but I've never given her the slightest reason to think it would ever be anything more than a working relationship again.'

She watched his face, her thoughts turning over and over.

'She told me you'd only taken me to bed because she was away in London! She told me you were always having flings with "two-bit actresses"!'

'Fantasies. Both.' He stepped towards her. 'I know what my reputation is like, but that's just because people like to believe that an unattached man in my position lives that sort of life. I can't claim an entirely unblemished past, but I've never been much interested in casual affairs. I'm not the type. And as for taking you to bed—nothing on heaven or earth could have stopped me that night, the way things were between us then.'

She swallowed, acutely aware of his physical presence close to her in the tiny living-room.

'You only had to ask me,' he said, and there was real pain in his voice. 'I would have told you the truth.'

'There's something else, something that Caroline said——'

'What was that?'

'She said you'd only made love to me for the sake of the film, because Dee Purvis was supposed to be in the throes of a passionate affair. She said that, because I was no actress, you knew you had to work on me to get me in the right state of mind——'

He swore furiously. 'That little schemer! When I get my hands on her——'

'But it's true, isn't it? Even back in Mauritius you

were working on me, trying to get me to feel more sensual and free?'

She challenged him with a direct look and he sat down on the edge of the sofa, sighing heavily.

'Bella, let's go back. Yes, it's true that I was, as you put it, working on you in Mauritius, but look at it from my point of view. There I was with everything lined up and ready to roll—and an actress who was as terrified and buttoned-up as someone's spinster aunt. I had to do something to loosen you up and I realised, pretty quickly, I'm afraid, that I seemed to be able to turn you on.' He darted her a quick grin, almost sheepish, at the admission. 'Then, that night on the beach, when I found you walking like a naked nymph from the waves, I knew it was too good an opportunity to miss. I wanted you to realise just how sensual and arousing you could be. But something started to happen to me then; I guess the roles started to reverse. I thought I was working on you, but what was really happening was that you were starting to work on me. Walking away from you there was the hardest thing I've ever done in my life, and from then on you began to work some sort of magic on me. I didn't mean to kiss you, that first time, but I just couldn't help myself. I had no intention at all of getting involved with you, but it began to happen anyway. By the time I left Mauritius I could hardly think about anything except when I was going to see you again.'

'But you left me! You left me that night when Caroline came to look for you, and you didn't come back.'

'No, I didn't. And I've already told you why. It was the end of a long and upsetting evening for you. I was worried I was just taking advantage of your vulnerability. And the last thing I wanted was for you to wake up the next day regretting you'd ever clapped eyes on me!'

'Is that really the only reason?'

'What possible other reason could there have been?'

'Caroline——'

'Caroline didn't come into it.'

She shook her head, puzzled. 'But I'm sure, on the beach, you let me think she was in your room——'

'If I did, it was only because I was trying to keep some sort of distance between us. I wanted you very badly, but you were so clearly not in the market for a one-night fling, and I was already getting nervous about the uncharted waters I seemed to be heading for.'

'You? Nervous?'

'Yes. Me.' He smiled at her, but his eyes were wary. 'I've always been in control of my own life, and I suddenly had this very strong instinct that it was slipping from my grasp. There was something so different about you, something I couldn't put my finger on, but I knew it felt serious and I wasn't at all sure I liked it.' He paused, his eyes roaming her face for a moment. 'Then, back in London, all I knew was that I was longing to see you again, those beautiful violet eyes of yours and that hesitant smile.' Colour crept into her pale face at the warmth of his eyes on hers. Then his smile faded. 'But when I found out what you and Mandy had been up to I simply felt furious. Doubly furious because, not only had I been made a complete fool of, and my work messed up, but the girl who'd done it was the one I'd been lying awake at nights dreaming about——'

She shook her head wildly. 'We just didn't think——'

'I know, I know!' He put up a hand to stop her words. 'Please let's not go into all that again. But all I knew at the time was that I had to get you back to put right the damage to the movie, even if I had to club you over the head and drag you there unconscious.'

'Which you practically did.'

He bent his head, examining the carpet, and when he spoke again there was a catch of laughter in his voice.

'Anger and lust are a very potent combination, especially when combined with acute jealousy! When I saw you on that platform delivering your lecture, so poised and confident and so utterly gorgeous, with all those other men slavering over you——'

'They weren't! They were serious scientists, interested in what I was saying!'

'Maybe that too,' he acknowledged, 'but anyway, one way and another, I felt almost out of my mind with the strength of my very mixed feelings towards you. Because the minute I saw you again—the real you, not the pretend Mandy—I knew I wanted you every bit as much, if not a hundred times more, than before. And that being so furious with you made no difference at all.'

She looked at him, loving him. 'It was the same for me,' she acknowledged, shyly. 'The same mixture. Except that I was angry that you'd made me look such a fool in front of all those people who matter in my world.'

He challenged her with a look. 'Then we've both managed to upset each other's work,' he pointed out quietly.

'Yes,' she acknowledged, meeting his eyes. 'We've made things very hard for each other.'

She heard him take in his breath sharply. 'In more

ways than one. I felt a malicious fate was at work when we had to spend the night out in the mountains! I think it was only acute exasperation that prevented me from ravishing you on the spot!'

She laughed in astonishment. 'You were sleeping like a top when I woke up!'

'All an act, Bella. I'd been lying awake for hours in a positive agony of frustration, desperately trying to preserve some decency between our prone forms. Which wasn't helped, incidentally, by the way you kept turning over and snuggling cosily into my arms!'

'I didn't!'

'Well, it wasn't me. Believe me, it wasn't me. I didn't trust myself that much! That's why I crashed out on you the next night, in such an ungentlemanly fashion—I'd hardly slept a wink the night before.'

She blushed as she confessed, 'I thought it was your film, again. I thought that night in the car you'd just decided to calm me down and butter me up, to get some good acting out of me. I always seem to think the worst of you.'

'Do you think you could change?' He cocked an eye at her.

'What do you mean?'

'I mean, if we still saw each other—could you think better of me?'

Then she understood what he was asking, and a cold pit seemed to open up in the bottom of her stomach. She stood up, slowly, like an old woman, and went to the window. It seemed chilly in the room, and she hugged herself with her arms. Outside were tiny figures hurrying along the pavement below, oblivious to her pain.

'No,' she whispered, so quietly that he barely heard.

'No?'

'No.'

Behind her she heard him thump the sofa in exasperation. 'What do I have to do, Bella? What would make you see me as a man instead of a monster?'

She squeezed her eyes tight shut. She did see him as a man, that was the whole trouble. She saw him as a man she loved, and desired, and wanted to be with all her life. And nothing less than that would do. He might want to prolong their affair for a while, but for her it was impossible. She would never stand the heartbreak and loss when he chose to move on elsewhere.

'You got it right in Wales,' she said tightly, 'You said it was just one of those things. That we were good together.' She whirled round, her voice twisting with pain. 'Well, you were right. We were "good together". If you want to know the truth, I've never felt anything like it in my life before! It was like being transported! But it's not enough for me on its own. There has to be something more than a physical relationship——'

In two strides he was across the room, gripping her wrists so tightly it hurt. His eyes blazed down at her. 'Who's talking about only a physical relationship?'

'You were! In Wales! If it had been anything more, you would have come to me—tried to straighten out all those misunderstandings.'

His gaze stripped across her face, his mouth cruel with tension. At his jaw she saw a pulse beating hard. 'Listen to me, Bella, and listen hard because I'm only going to say this once.' The words rapped out of him like bullets from a gun. 'You're right about Wales. I didn't know what was happening between us, I only knew I wanted to hold you more than I'd ever wanted any woman in my arms before! That got in the way of everything, any rational thinking. If I thought at all, it was, I admit, on the lines that you said. I thought it was going to be a brilliant affair, a wonderful explosion of passion that would last maybe days, maybe weeks, maybe months—I didn't know, and I didn't care. I just wanted to live it.'

His eyes blazed down on hers. 'I always thought my work was my life, and that anything else had to take second place. And I was working like a trouper to finish shooting on time. So, when you gave me the cold shoulder as you did, I tried to rationalise it all away. I told myself it would have ended anyway, in due course, and that, while it was a pity it had ended so quickly and so badly, it was probably for the best in the long run.

'That's why I didn't pursue you, or try to set the record straight—I turned to drink instead.' He grimaced bitterly. 'I told myself I didn't want you to get hurt, but it was really me I was trying to protect. It was useless, Bella. I've been moping about like a bear with a sore head ever since you left Wales. Everything has seemed flat and empty and meaningless—even my work, which I thought was my very life's blood!'

Her eyes widened, trying to take in the scope of what he was saying.

'Bella, I always thought of myself as a loner, footloose and rootless. But now I feel cast adrift. I've been so miserable over the past few weeks that I haven't known where to put myself. I can't eat, I can't work, I can't sleep. Every time I close my eyes all I can see is you!' He grimaced at his own weakness. 'What would your diagnosis be, Dr Latham?'

'I'm not a doctor,' she managed to get out, 'not until I finish my PhD,' but the words were choking in her throat with the slow fire of joy that was beginning to smoulder inside her.

'I'd say I was in love,' he said bluntly.

'In love?' she echoed, with foolish disbelief.

'I love you, Bella. I can't function without you. I haven't come here to ask you to revive our brief affair. I couldn't stand that insecurity. I want to live with you, marry you, be with you always——'

'Marry?' Shock seemed to have robbed her of her wits, and her voice was wooden.

He took her shock wrongly, his face hardening. 'Look, I'm under no illusions. I know it's a lousy offer. I'll always be unfaithful. No——' he put up a hand when he saw her horrified look '——I don't mean with other women. I could never do that. I mean with my work. It's a punishing mistress. It rules my life. I'd never get home at a regular hour, and I'd always be flying off to distant places for weeks at a stretch, and when things went wrong I'd get mean and moody and be hell to live with——'

'Stop it! Stop it!' Bella threw herself into his arms, laughing and crying with shock. Inside her heart threatened to burst with happiness. 'You're sounding like your own worst enemy. I'd hate a man who arrived home every night at six, and expected his supper on the table. I couldn't live with anyone like that. My work's important to me, too. I'd have to have the time and space to carry on with it.'

His arms tightened round her. 'Is that a yes? Could you love me, Bella?'

'Could——? Oh, I think I have almost always, right since that first day. You set me free from my past. Until I met you, I thought I was destined to stay single all my life.'

His lips met hers. 'I didn't mean to say all this,' he

groaned. 'I was only going to be cautious, test the water, ask if you could bear to come to the première with me.'

He kissed her again, deeply, completely, his hands moulding her back through her robe. 'Can we go back to bed? I know it's not the best of times but, even if I can't make love to you, I want to hold you close.'

Later, a long time later, he asked her, 'When you thought you were pregnant, how did you feel?'

'I was shocked at first, but later I realised I wanted it. I wanted your baby more than anything else in the world.'

'Then we'll have to see what we can do,' he smiled deeply, 'after I've been thoroughly selfish and had you to myself for a time!'

'And I'm a very practical person,' she added. 'I'd already begun to work out how much maternity leave I could take, and whether the institute would let me go back part time.'

'I know you are.' He kissed her, his beautiful eyes warm with love. 'I know you are. Shall I tell you when I first began to have an inkling about how I really felt about you? It was when I walked into that conference room in Bristol, full of fury, and saw you coolly take the stage and devastate everyone in the room. Brains and beauty mixed! That was when I first saw the real you, and it floored me completely.'

'When I glimpsed you there I just felt terrified,' she admitted. 'Terrified because I knew you were angry with me, but also because of how I felt. No man's ever made me tremble before, just by looking at me.'

Outside the light was already fading. Bella stretched her arms luxuriously on the pillows. 'This is terrible. It's almost evening and we still haven't got up.'

He ran his hand lovingly down her side. 'Can you think of a better way of passing a damp autumn Saturday?'

She shook her head, smiling. 'No.'

'Can we do it often?'

'Every week.' Her eyes danced. 'Except, of course, when you're filming!'

'I somehow think my schedules are going to get a lot more relaxed in the future!'

'Not if the première's a wild success.' Contented, she curled into his arms. 'Luke, can I ask you a favour?'

He smiled deeply at her. 'Do you think I could deny you anything?'

'Good—because you might not like it.'

Three weeks later Bella sat at home, feet up on the sofa, a sandwich on her lap, a pile of papers at her feet. She'd done a good evening's work and now she was watching the news bulletin, more happy and relaxed than she had ever been in her life.

On the screen the picture flicked to London's West End, to show the royal Prince and Princess stepping from their limousine to attend a major charity film première. And suddenly there was Mandy, smiling at the Prince and curtsying deeply.

Bella's heart swelled with pride. Her sister looked stunning in her flamboyant silver gown, every inch the rising star everyone was predicting she would be, while at her side was Luke, tall, dark and devastatingly handsome in his formal evening wear.

She loved him for his generosity in forgiving Mandy, and being glad to let her share the show-business limelight with him. She loved everything about him, and she hugged her knees hard in delight.

And as the camera panned over him she saw him flash a quick, brooding smile out of the screen, just for her, and her heart began to beat a private tattoo of excitement and anticipation at the thought that in just a few hours he would be coming home to her, and gathering her into his arms yet again.

HARLEQUIN
Romance

**This June, travel to Turkey
with Harlequin Romance's**

**THE JEWELS OF HELEN
by Jane Donnelly**

She was a spoiled brat who liked her own way.

Eight years ago Max Torba thought Anni was self-centered—
and that she didn't care if her demands made life impossible
for those who loved her.

Now, meeting again at Max's home in Turkey, it was clear he
still held the same opinion, no matter how hard she tried to
make a good impression. "You haven't changed much, have
you?" he said. "You still don't give a damn for the trouble you
cause."

But did Max's opinion really matter? After all, Anni had no
intention of adding herself to his admiring band of female
followers....

HARLEQUIN
American Romance

RELIVE THE MEMORIES....

All the way from turn-of-the-century Ellis Island to the future of the nineties...A CENTURY OF AMERICAN ROMANCE takes you on a nostalgic journey through the twentieth century.

This May, watch for the final title of A CENTURY OF AMERICAN ROMANCE—#389 A > LOVERBOY, Judith Arnold's lighthearted look at love in 1998!

Don't miss a day of A CENTURY OF AMERICAN ROMANCE

A CENTURY OF
AMERICAN ROMANCE
1990s

The women...the men...the passions...the memories...

HARLEQUIN Temptation

Give in to Temptation! Harlequin Temptation

The story of a woman who knows her own mind, her own heart . . . and of the man who touches her, body and soul.

Intimate, sexy stories of today's woman—her troubles, her triumphs, her tears, her laughter.

And her ultimate commitment to love.

Four new titles each month—get 'em while they're hot. Available wherever paperbacks are sold. <small>Temp-1</small>

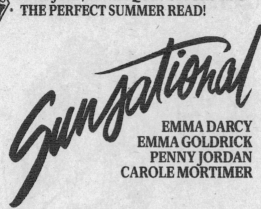

Harlequin Superromance®

Here are the longer, more involving stories you have been waiting for . . . Superromance.

Modern, believable novels of love, full of the complex joys and heartaches of real people.

Intriguing conflicts based on today's constantly changing life-styles.

Four new titles every month.
